GETAWAY BAY SINGLES

GETAWAY BAY RESORT ROMANCE, BOOK 8

ELANA JOHNSON

feel-good fiction

ELANA JOHNSON

ISBN-13: 978-1-63876-017-7

ONE

KATHERINE HARRISON SIGHED as she sat down, her bowl of chicken noodle soup rotating in the microwave behind her. The break room at Clean Sweep needed a thorough cleaning, ironic considering this was a maid service.

The biggest, best maid service on the island of Getaway Bay. With a dirty break room. As the owner of the company, she should clean it, but she couldn't get up the energy to do much more than swipe right on her phone as she looked at her dating app.

Getaway Bay Singles promised to be the "directional compass in your dating life" much like a GPS was to help someone get around the island. GBS boasted high percentages of singles getting together and staying together right here on the island, and Katie had decided to join the service because she was tired of managing the seventeen people at Clean Sweep and then going home to take care of her ten-year-old daughter.

Heather was awesome, and Katie didn't mind being a mother or a business owner. She was just lonely. So lonely.

And GBS helped with that, so she was glad she'd joined though she hadn't made much of a love connection yet. She tapped and swiped through the app, reading quick sentence like *AndrewB and JoanS went to Spam Hut*, and *MikeT and TerriL enjoyed an island tour.*

GBS helped with restaurants, date ideas, and more. She'd filled out all of her favorites the first night she'd downloaded the app, staying up well past her bedtime to do so. But if she ever were to meet a man in real life from the app, she felt certain they'd have an excellent meal at a restaurant they both liked. The app would not lead them astray, that much Katie knew.

She'd been chatting with a man named TeddyF for several days, and a message from him popped up on her screen. Surviving the week?

Sort of, she typed back to him, a smile brightening her face and her day. *Sooo busy this week.*

Cleaning, right? his next message said.

Right. Katie had told him about herself, as many as the surface things as she felt comfortable with. Favorite movie, favorite food, what she liked to do in her spare time. The thought of spare time was actually laughable, but she wasn't laughing.

She had one more thing to tell him before she'd be comfortable getting together with him, and she set her phone down as she thought through their few weeks of conversation. She liked him. He was witty and smart. Thoughtful and inquisitive. He'd been kind, and while his profile picture was a cartoon rendition of him, she thought he was probably attractive, in an older, closer-to-fifty silver fox kind of way.

Because Katie had faced it—she wasn't exactly a spring chicken at age forty-six.

TeddyF liked Chinese food, and warm island rain, and the view from the highest point in Getaway Bay. He worked in the technology sector as an app developer. He'd only been on the island for thirteen months, and he claimed he hadn't had a serious relationship in years and years.

One or two dates is all, he'd told her. *And then the spark is gone.*

When she'd asked him if he was looking for serious, he'd given her one word: *Yes.*

And while Katie had had serious twice now, she had to admit she didn't want to move into her fifties and then sixties by herself.

I have something to tell you, she typed, her fingers moving in a methodical and slow way. *And you can take your time responding. Think about it. All of that.*

Oh, boy, he said. *All right. Go ahead.*

I have a ten-year-old daughter named Heather. Katie stared at the words. She'd only told three men on GBS about Heather, and all three of them had cooled considerably afterward. But honestly, did they think they were courting a forty-six-year-old woman without any ties or responsibilities?

TeddyF was forty-nine, at least according to his profile. She'd learned that most men didn't lie on GBS. There wasn't really a point, as it was an app for singles in a very limited location, not across-the-ocean correspondence.

Am I meant to guess the thing you need to tell me? ;)

Katie startled at the ding and resulting vibration in her hands from his message. A light laugh tickled her vocal cords, and she tapped on the arrow to send her sentence through the magic of the WiFi to TeddyF's phone.

Then she flipped her phone over and pushed her chair back. She realized in that moment and with that motion that she didn't want TeddyF to cool considerably after he found out about Heather. She didn't want that at all, and if he asked to meet her, she'd say yes.

"You should ask him," she said aloud just as Lacey entered the break room.

"What?" She pulled open the fridge and pulled out a can of Diet Coke—her lunch.

"Just talking to myself again," Katie said as her phone chimed once, twice, three times.

"Ooh, someone's popular." Lace sat down beside Katie and grinned. "Is that GBS?"

"How did you know?"

"That notification sound is unique."

"Are you using the app?"

"Who doesn't?" Lace shrugged and took a swig of her soda. "So, who's the guy? Are you meeting him?"

"Thinking about it," Katie said, telling her office manager the truth. If there was someone who cared about Clean Sweep as much as Katie, it was Lacey Moon, and she'd been with Katie since the beginning.

She'd also been as unlucky in love, and Katie said, "Have you ever met up with someone on GBS?"

"Yeah, a couple of times." She tossed her dark ponytail over her shoulder. "The app is pretty amazing and matching up what the two of you like and suggesting the type of date you're likely to enjoy."

"That's what I've heard." Katie's phone *bllliing*ed again, but she still didn't dare pick it up.

"You want me to see what he's saying?"

Katie covered her phone with her hand. "No...." She looked at Lace, a flicker of fear rumbling through her. "I just told him about Heather."

"Oh."

Yeah, that one word said it all, and Katie nodded, her palm still flat against the plastic case of her phone. She drew in a deep breath and said, "Here I go."

Ten years old, Teddy had said. *That's great. My youngest nephew is ten. Great age.*

I like kids, if that's what you're wondering.

And then, his last message was *Did I lose you?*

She looked up at Lace. "He said he likes kids." She wasn't sure why, but her voice held a measure of awe. "What should I do?"

"Ask him out." Lace grinned and finished her can of pop.

"Really? Just like that."

"Just. Like. That." She really hit that last T, and Katie felt the vibrations of it down inside her stomach. Which may not be as flat as it once had been. Maybe she could get together with TeddyF in a couple of weeks, after she'd had a chance to hit it hard on the treadmill, really get that ten pounds off she'd been slowly putting on since moving to paradise and eating more fresh fruit smoothies than was humanly sane.

After all, fruit had calories too. As did the coconut milk and sugar added to the smoothies that made them so delicious.

"Okay," she said, letting her fingers fly over the screen. "I'm going to do it."

Want to get together sometime? She read the sentence aloud to Lace and waited for the thirty-something to give her approval. When she nodded, Katie hit send.

Absolutely, Teddy said almost instantly. *What are you doing tonight?*

"Tonight?" The disbelief in Katie's voice felt like a lead weight in her lungs. "He wants to get together tonight."

"Great," Lace said, snatching the phone from Katie's fingers. "You're free, right?"

"I need someone to watch Heather."

Lace gave her a semi-disgusted look. "Duh. I'll do it. It's Friday night. You should go out with this...TeddyF. Oh, he's hot."

"His profile picture is a cartoon."

"Yeah, and he's gorgeous, even as an animated head." Lace's thumbs tippity-tapped, and she grinned as she hit send and handed the phone back.

Katie almost didn't dare to look at it. "What did you say?"

"Read it."

Katie rolled her eyes and said, "Doing nothing tonight.

Let me see if I can get a sitter." She glanced at Lace. "I'm tired."

"And you're never going to meet the man of your dreams if you take a nap every Friday night."

"It's not every Friday night," Katie grumbled as her phone blinged at her.

I hope you can. I'd love to meet you.

A warmth started in her stomach and radiated outward to all of her limbs. She could make him wait ten minutes before saying she'd found someone to babysit. So she did.

———

Katie sat at an outside table, her heeled foot tapping while she waited. She wasn't being impatient—Teddy wasn't late yet. No, it was nervous energy that had her heel clicking against the stones with the rhythm of a metronome.

Heather had homework, but Katie never made her do it on Friday nights. So there'd been absolutely no reason why she couldn't go on this date, and while she didn't really want to cancel, the anxiety over the unknown had her wishing she'd put on a wig and a giant pair of sunglasses before coming to the bistro.

She fingered the ends of her hair, which she'd actually let down out of its customary ponytail, the curl it held naturally quite nice when she wasn't trying to keep it out of the toilet. She'd let Lace switch out the black cardigan for a bright red one, but with the blue and white dress, she felt more like the American flag than a woman ever should.

Every man who walked by sent her heartbeat into a tizzy, but none of them veered into Bora Bora's. Seven o'clock came and then went, and still Teddy hadn't shown up.

The three minutes she waited felt like three years, and then someone said, "Katie?" in a deep, luxurious voice that reminded her of melted chocolate and marshmallows.

It also sounded very much like... "Theo?" She turned, sure she would not come face-to-face with her ex-husband.

That couldn't happen.

But she stared right into the blazing blue eyes of Theodore Fleming himself. Very much an older version of the man she'd married twenty-five years ago. She blinked, wanting to rub her eyes with her fists.

"Theo?" she said again, half-hopeful that he wouldn't remember her. Which was the most foolish thing she'd ever thought. Of course he'd remember her. They'd shared a house and a bed and a life together for five years.

His eyes widened, and he fell back a step. "Katherine?"

She had enough time to take in the gorgeous quality of his silver hair, still with some of that dark brown in there. My, he'd aged very well. Very well, indeed. Those eyes hadn't changed, nor had the fact that he kept his face absolutely clean-shaven.

He wore a black pair of slacks that looked like they'd cost as much as her mortgage, and a cornflower blue polo that accentuated his chest and upper arms. He certainly hadn't put on ten pounds in the past few years, and Katie wanted to flee very, very badly.

"I can't believe you're going by Teddy now," she said

with a hint of acid in her voice. He'd never used that nickname in all the years she'd known him. But of course, one of the reasons they'd gotten divorced was because she hadn't known him at all.

"Just on GBS," he said easily, like seeing her after two decades hadn't affected him at all. Had he ever thought about her? Did he even miss her after she'd declared him having an affair with his obsession to start his own business and walked out?

"It gives me a certain sense of…anonymity." He flashed a smile that definitely held some nerves, and Katie was glad for that. "You never went by Katie."

"Well, I do now," she said, remembering her early twenties when Katherine carried more dignity, and Katie was for little girls.

He pulled out the chair like he would sit and stay. Horror snaked through her. "Mind if I sit?"

"I'm surprised you want to."

He did and gazed at her, an unreadable expression on that handsome face. She'd give Theo that. He'd always been charming and handsome. She'd never doubted him, or the fact that he'd own and operate a very successful business one day. She just didn't want to come second or third or sometimes last to his whims, ideas, dreams, and career.

"So," he said. "Where did the Harrison come from?"

TWO

THEODORE FLEMING COULD NOT BELIEVE he was sitting at a table across from his ex-wife. Simply could not believe it. At the same time, he didn't want to be anywhere else. He'd enjoyed talking to Katie all these weeks, and while it might take a day or two for him to actually think of her as Katie and not Katherine, he thought it was an adjustment he could make.

He'd asked her about her unfamiliar last name, and she was still staring at him. A waiter appeared and said, "Do you guys know what you'd like to drink? Or do you need another minute?"

"I'll have water with a lot of lemon," he said, barely glancing up at the man.

A smile touched Katie's lips, but Theo couldn't tell if it was borne of disgust or fondness. "Still the same." She looked up at the waiter. "I'll have the frozen peach smoothie."

If Theo would've been tasked with ordering for her, he probably would've landed on that. Or at least he'd like to think he would've. He hadn't seen Katie in twenty years, so maybe there was more to her that had changed than just her name.

Of course there is, he told himself, keeping his eyes on her face though he'd already seen her more womanly curves. She'd aged, obviously, but she was still as beautiful and sexy as the twenty-two-year-old he'd met on the campus of Texas A&M, as the bride he'd kissed to make his wife, as the English major who'd supported him by teaching high school while he tried to get his start-up to well, start up.

The waiter walked away, and Theo picked up the menu. He'd only been in Getaway Bay for just over a year, and he hadn't been to this particular bistro yet. He hadn't apologized for being late yet, because the shock of seeing his ex-wife sitting at the table where they'd agreed to meet was still coursing through him.

He obviously couldn't start dating her.

Could he?

She must've gotten married again, hence the new last name he hadn't recognized, as well as the ten-year-old daughter.

Theo's pulse hopped over itself, but he stayed at the table. Katie's daughter didn't bother Theo, though he'd never been a father and didn't know how to deal with children for longer than a few hours. If there was one thing Theo had learned in his life, it was that he could figure things out. If given enough time and opportunity, he could learn what he needed to in order to be successful.

Could he do that with Katie and her daughter?

Something inside him told him to wish her well and go on home. But a louder voice urged him to stay, find out what she'd been up to all this time, and share some personal things about himself.

She'd finally left when his second business had tanked, leaving them destitute and without many prospects of ever being above the poverty line. If Katie knew about his bank account now, he wondered what would change between them.

"So," he said, very aware he started a lot of sentences like that. "Do you want to stay?" She had ordered a smoothie. "I mean, I'll understand if you'd rather just go home and then delete me from your contacts on GBS."

He really hoped she wouldn't stand and storm away, and when she didn't a bit of hope entered his bloodstream. But not much, because she wasn't talking either.

So he would. "I've never been re-married," he said, not quite sure why he started there. "A lot has happened, I suppose, but I stayed in Texas until moving here."

"Why'd you come here?" she asked, and Theo was glad her vocal cords had thawed.

"Business," he said, which was true, if only partially. He'd heard of the billionaire club here on this island, and he wanted to find out if it really existed. When he'd confirmed the Nine-0 Club—and been invited to join it—he'd left the Lone Star State, somewhere he'd lived for almost fifty years.

He did miss the sagebrush and the insane football traditions, the barbecue and the threat of hurricanes. But Getaway Bay had tropical storms too, so he supposed that was the same.

"Something with technology," she said. "Isn't that what you messaged me?"

"Yes," he said, wondering if he should tell her the whole story now or in little pieces as they continued to see each other. Just the fact that he thought she'd go out with him again was pure insanity. She probably wouldn't even order dinner. "App development," he added. "It's just a lot of code, honestly."

"I didn't realize you were into computer science."

"Well, that came after you left." He didn't mean for the words to leave his mouth with such bite, but they did. "I'm sorry," he said quickly. "That was...rude."

She cocked her head, her hair falling softly over her shoulders in a way that brought decades-old memories soaring to the surface of his mind. "Did you actually miss me after I left?"

"Truthfully?" he asked.

"I'd like to know the truth, yes."

"Then yes, terribly. It was...." He cleared his throat, some of the suppressed memories quite unpleasant. "Difficult. My life was very difficult without you." He wasn't sure he needed to qualify in all the ways he'd missed her.

But he had. He'd missed having her presence in the apartment where they lived. He missed having her to bounce ideas off of. He missed holding her hand and kissing her forehead while his mind worked through some unknown problem with whatever he was working on. He missed having her reassurance that he'd figure out what to do with his life, and that she'd be right there with him once he did.

That might have been the biggest thing she'd taken when she'd left. Without her, he lost all his confidence. How he'd found it again, he wasn't quite sure.

But the world had changed in twenty years. Technology had grown and expanded and returning to college to earn a computer science degree had been logical.

"I went back to school," he said. "Got a degree in computer science and started working for a big video game company out of Dallas."

She nodded, her eyes alive and bright, indicating that she was listening.

"And I dabbled in building my own things here and there," he said. "I launched Software Solutions about five years ago, but it wasn't until about two years ago that I moved into app development."

He was aware that she probably had no idea what he was talking about, so the cute confusion on her face wasn't unexpected.

"Basically, I created a program that makes business owners able to make their own apps at a low cost," he said. "So if say, a gardening company wants to offer their customers an app where they can schedule lawn mowing or order supplies with the tap of a button, they buy my software. It's drag and drop, super user friendly, and we manage all the technical stuff for them."

She leaned forward, interest parading through her eyes now. "Could a cleaning company do that?"

"Of course. Set up times for when maids would go out, cancel service right on your phone, leave reviews, request a cleaning—even a specific person." He stopped talking, understanding dawning on him. "Do you have an app, Kather—Katie?"

"No," she said, leaning back as the waiter appeared with a glass easily as tall as his head, filled to the brim with light orange liquid and a huge puff of whipped cream on top. He set the concoction in front of Katie, and put the water and a bowl full of lemons near Theo.

"Thank you," he murmured, still quite enamored with this woman he used to know.

"Are you ready to order?" the waiter asked, and Theo picked up the menu.

"I haven't even looked yet," he said. "Can we get a few more minutes?"

"Of course."

Theo pretended to look through his choices, though he couldn't get his mind to settle. He'd simply ask for the best thing on the menu once the waiter returned, as he liked almost anything.

Katie set her menu down only a moment after him, and he was once again struck at her beauty, the way her aquamarine eyes seemed to drink him up and radiate warmth at the same time.

"Still averse to carbonated beverages?" She wrapped her lips around her straw, and Theo felt the temperature shoot through the roof.

He stared for a second past comfortable, and then cleared his throat, actually reaching up to loosen his tie before realizing he wasn't wearing one. He rarely left the house without a dress shirt and tie on, fancy slacks, and patent leather shoes.

"Yes," he finally pushed out of a dry throat. He reached for the lemon wedges and selected one, almost throwing it at Katie because it was so slippery. He got a good grip on it and squeezed it into his water. "It gets worse the older I get."

"Yeah, have you hit fifty yet?" Her gaze drifted to his gray hair, and Theo was actually used to this type of behavior from women. Since his hair had started to lose its color, he'd gotten more female attention. Still hadn't gone out with the same woman more than three times since arriving in Getaway Bay, though.

"You know I haven't," he said. "Don't tell me you've forgotten my birthday."

She shrugged, which meant *no* in Katherine Fleming language, and Theo found it downright adorable.

Stop it, he told himself. There was no way he'd be getting a second date with his ex-wife, let alone making a real relationship with her. But they did both live in Getaway Bay, and what were the chances of that?

"Tell me about Heather," he said next, spying the waiter coming out of the corner of his eye. He'd know for sure if Katie was going to stay if she ordered food.

Before she could give him even a single sentence about her daughter, the waiter arrived. Katie ordered the steamed mussels as an appetizer and then the surf and turf. "Medium," she said, handing the menu back to the waiter.

Theo couldn't help the enormous grin that sat on his mouth as he said, "What's the best thing here?"

———

"So how was the date last night?"

Theo looked up from his phone, where he'd been trying to employ his Superman heat vision to make KatieH message him on GBS. Unfortunately, he didn't have super-powers, and she hadn't responded to his message from last night.

She'd said a few things about her daughter—Heather liked to paint, she loved guacamole and chips, and she took in every stray cat that wandered by their house. But she really kept the conversation on building an app, and what that would take.

Theo had gotten much better at listening to those around him since his marriage to Katie, and after their date had ended—two and a half hours after it had begun—he'd messaged her from the comfort of his high-rise condo overlooking East Bay.

I can help you build an app for your cleaning company, if you'd like.

In fact, he may have sketched out a few features she'd definitely want that morning before coming into the office.

And his office was a second apartment he'd purchased one floor down, and the only other person who ever came in was Ben Brown, who was also

GETAWAY BAY SINGLES   19

standing in front of him, wanting to know about the date.

"What?" Theo asked.

"I've been in here for ten minutes, giving you the weekly update from Dallas, and you haven't looked at me once." Ben grinned and sat in the chair across from Theo. "So, who was she?"

Theo didn't want to say, but he couldn't help the giddy feeling in his chest. "This is going to sound crazy," he said.

"Oh, I can't wait." Ben's dark eyes glittered, and while they only worked for an hour on Saturday mornings, the man had never complained. He'd come to Getaway Bay with Theo, and he'd managed to find a girlfriend within the first thirty days. Even though that relationship had only lasted a couple of months, he'd been out with more women since than Theo had been out with in years.

"It was my ex-wife," Theo said, leaning away from his desk and thus his phone. "And I thought she'd get up and walk right out, but she didn't. She stayed and ordered lobster and steak and we talked."

"Talked," Ben repeated, folding his arms.

"Yes," Theo said with a bit of defensiveness in his tone. "Talked."

"You didn't kiss her?"

"I don't kiss everyone I go out with," he said. "It was our first date."

"You kissed that English woman, what? Three weeks ago? First date and everything."

"Yes, well." Theo cleared his throat. "Felicity was a bit of a tart, wasn't she?" Very good at flirting and asking questions, and they'd chatted for hours through GBS for only three days before meeting in person.

And fine, there'd been a kiss—and then she'd disappeared.

Theo hadn't known what he'd done wrong. Ben, who was fifteen years younger than Theo's forty-nine, said some women just liked to go out once. "One and done," he'd called it.

"So the ex-wife," Ben said. "Katherine."

"She goes by Katie now."

"Ohh, I bet she does." Ben chuckled as Theo's phone zinged out the sound that meant someone had messaged him through GBS. Sometimes he really hated that sound, and he wondered what it would take for his chief engineers to change it.

But this time, the sound made his heart leapfrog around inside his chest like he'd swallowed one of the amphibians while it was still alive.

Please be KatieH, he thought as he reached for his phone. After all, sometimes his employees messaged him through the app to test things, or just to get his attention as he was notoriously bad with email.

But this message was from Katie, and she said, *I'd like that*.

Theo said, "A-ha!" and punched the air in triumph. He turned his phone toward Ben. "I just got a second date."

Ben leaned forward, his eyes scanning the conversation. "And another customer."

That too, but Theo was mostly interested in the date.

THREE

KATIE SAT at her kitchen table the following morning, her calendar out in front of her. Heather stood in the kitchen, whisking together pancakes. "Mom, can I heat up the syrup in the bottle?"

"Yes," she said without looking up.

"Because last time it sort of exploded."

Exploded got Katie's attention, and she looked away from the mess of cramped writing on the desk calendar in front of her. "What?"

"I think I just need to pop the lid, but then it leaks, because the bottle's too tall." She set down her whisk and looked at her mom.

Katie loved how her daughter had the same round face she did. The exact same shade of brown hair. But while Katie had blue-green eyes, Heather had her father's eyes. Ray's had been a bit darker, but Heather had a lighter version, with a hint of green if she stood in the sunlight just right.

She loved cooking, and since Katie wasn't aspiring to be a chef, she let Heather make whatever she wanted, buying random ingredients like saffron or sesame oil on her way home from work.

"Maybe pour some syrup into a glass measuring cup," Katie suggested.

"Okay, I'll do that." Heather turned and bent, struggling to get the griddle out of the cupboard. Katie went back to her calendar though her GBS app blinged at her again.

If it was Theo…she still couldn't believe she'd stayed for dinner last night. Not only that, she'd *enjoyed* herself. A lot.

Theo had always been charming, she'd give him that. The truth was, he'd always been the North pole of a magnet while she was the South. She was attracted to him even after all these years, and the conversation hadn't been difficult. The food was delicious, and they'd left on pleasant terms.

He hadn't asked her out again, but he had messaged her to ask if she needed help building an app for her cleaning company.

Yes, she very much needed help with that.

She hadn't answered him back yet, because she knew what he was really asking. If she said yes, they'd have to see each other again. If she said no, she'd basically be telling him to delete her as a contact on GBS and start over.

Katie focused on scheduling Anna for the next two

weeks, printing in neat, tidy letters in the dark green pen assigned to the maid. If she could just have fifteen more minutes without an interruption, she'd have everything ready for the next two weeks.

Eleven minutes into the schedule, the doorbell rang. A moment later, Claire stepped into the house. "It's just me." She walked down the hall and into the kitchen and dining room, where Heather and Katie worked.

"Hey, Claire," Heather said. "These are hot. You want to eat?"

"Hey, baby." Katie heard the fondness in her friend's voice. "Your mom's not eating?"

"Five minutes," Katie barked out, determined to finish before she did anything else. Yes, her stomach was roaring for food. No, she wouldn't die.

She finished as quickly as she could and joined Heather and Claire at the counter, taking two pancakes from the stack and slathering butter on them. "These look great, Heather." She smiled at her daughter. She'd been making pancakes since she was seven, and her first batch had been too blonde and rather doughy inside. But these were perfectly brown, as well as light and fluffy.

"Did you ask your mom about her date last night?" Claire met Katie's eyes over Heather's head, a knowing look in her eye.

Katie shook her head, but Heather said, "Not yet. How was it, Mom?"

"Oh, it was okay," she said.

"You going to see him again?" Claire asked.

"Why are you sitting here eating pancakes? Don't you

have bathrooms to clean?" Katie glared at her best friend and maid, half joking but half serious too.

Claire simply laughed and took another bite of her pancake. "She must like him," she said around bread and syrup. "Otherwise she'd tell us she wasn't going to go out with him again."

"He's an app developer," Katie said slowly. "And I'm thinking Clean Sweep needs an app."

Claire blinked, her bright blue eyes curious. "Are you kidding? That would be awesome."

"Yeah, The—the man I met for dinner last night gave me some ideas."

"So you're going to see him again." Claire finished her pancakes and picked up her plate, taking it to the sink and rinsing it.

Katie exhaled heavily. "I'm not sure." She wished she didn't have ten-year-old ears in the room so she could really tell Claire who she'd met at Bora Bora and why she really wanted a second date with the magnetic Theo Fleming.

"Well, if it's good for the business...." Claire shrugged and continued doing the dishes. She did laundry too, and Katie was never happier than on Saturdays after Claire left. A clean house. A conversation with her friend. And a couple of days off until she had to face running her business again.

Katie did want Clean Sweep to continue to thrive. Grow, even. It had started with her and Claire, a dream, and more hard work than Katie had known how to do at the time.

She knew now, and she'd gained some respect for Theo and what he'd been trying to do during those five years of their marriage.

So she picked up her phone and typed out, *I'd like that,* and sent it to Theo.

A smiley face came back several moments later, and then *What are you doing this afternoon?*

Did he not remember she had a daughter? And her time with Heather was precious, especially on weekends.

Not available until Monday, she said. *And preferably during the day. Maybe lunch?*

The Theo she remembered sometimes skipped meals if he was knee-deep inside an idea.

Lunch on Monday sounds great. Should we let GBS choose for us again?

Katie had liked Bora Bora, just as her app had predicted she would. So she said, *Sure,* and asked Heather if she had any homework.

"Yeah, let me go get it," she said, leaving her plate on the counter.

"After you're done, we can go to the movies," Katie called after her. "Or the beach." It was the end of September and still plenty warm to lie on the sand and play in the ocean.

"Beach," Heather called back, always one to choose the outdoors over staying inside. Another characteristic she'd picked up from her father. Katie let her thoughts linger on Ray for a moment, and then she subdued them.

Just like Theo, it did no good to dwell on things—and people—she couldn't change. While she waited for

Heather to come back, she wondered if Theo had changed enough over the past twenty-five years to warrant starting another relationship with him.

Not a friendship.

Katie wasn't stupid, and she knew if she and Theo were to be anything, it would extend far past friendship. Her heart bumped around erratically, and she wondered if it had ever truly healed from the divorce all those years ago.

Probably not.

She picked up her phone and saw a few more messages from Theo. She read over them quickly, but they weren't anything that needed a fast response. So she silenced her phone, determined not to spend every waking moment from now until lunch on Monday thinking about her ex-husband.

Yeah, right. She didn't think that was possible, especially when Claire said, "So, you really did like this guy, right?" She looked up from Katie's phone, where she'd obviously been reading the messages.

Katie swiped the phone out of Claire's hand and said, "Hey," wanting to deny her interest in the TeddyF on her app.

In the end, her shoulders slumped. "Yeah," she sighed out. "I really like him. But Claire, it's insane. Like, absolutely insane. You won't believe who he is."

Claire paused in wiping down the counter, obviously hearing the emotion in Katie's voice.

"Why?" she asked. "Who is he?"

"My ex—"

"Okay," Heather said. "I only have two pages of math and then I have to read for thirty minutes."

"Okay," Katie said brightly, noting that Claire was still frozen in place. "Which do you want to do first?"

"Read." She dropped her math workbook on the counter and kept her library book in her hand. "Can I read on the couch?"

"As long as you stay out of Claire's way." Katie stood, taking her phone with her. "She has floors to do today."

And yet Claire still didn't move. Katie moved around the island and opened the fridge like she wanted something more to drink.

"Your ex-what?" Claire asked, her mouth barely moving.

"Husband," Katie whispered, reaching for the orange juice "The one who's not in prison."

Claire made a squeaking noise, and Katie felt about the same way.

———

She spent a glorious autumn weekend with her daughter, mostly on the beach and then in the backyard, which she kept meticulous and as green as possible. She loved the way she could prune a bush or tree and shape it into what she wanted. She loved the simple way nature took over if it was allowed, and she loved the way her daughter put out bowls and bowls of food and water for the homeless cats in the neighborhood.

But Monday came, as it always did, and Katie dropped

Heather at school before heading over to Clean Sweep. She posted the schedule for the next two weeks, something she wouldn't have to do physically if she had an app her employees could check.

She made a mental note to ask Theo if the app could have two sides—one for customers and one for employees, so her maids could get a notification when a new job came in. Then, knowing that her mental note-taking system had started failing about a decade ago, she pulled out her phone and typed out a quick question in a blank email.

There was no rule saying that this lunch couldn't be a business lunch. In fact, if she thought about it like that, her stomach didn't do a strange, twisting dance that made her feel like throwing up.

Her GBS bleeped, the sound it made when a recommendation was made, and she swiped it open to see that the app was leading her and Theo to lunch at Manni's taco stand on the beach. Fair enough. She loved fish tacos, and a lunch date was generally more casual than dinner.

She tapped the thumbs up icon and retreated to her office. She'd texted everyone working today what their schedule was, and she also had a job that day, cleaning a widow's house that sat up on the hill.

Then, it was on to lunch.

Katie was exceptionally good at compartmentalizing, and she put the lunch in the tidy little box where it belonged. Until then, she could only imagine what Theo would be wearing when he showed up to lunch.

FOUR

THEO KEPT one hand in his pocket as he strolled along the beachwalk from his condo building to the taco stand, which sat on the other side of East Bay. He'd dined there more times than he could count, and he hadn't been surprised that his app had suggested it for a midweek lunch date.

Businessmen, moms, and more ate at Manni's for lunch, and he scanned the crowd for Katie's beautiful face. A breeze blew in off the bay, ruffling his hair and the tails of his jacket. He panicked for a bit, thinking perhaps he should've left the jacket at the office.

But it was a sport jacket, thrown on over a T-shirt. It was casual, as Ben had said. Not that Theo had asked his best friend and business partner for his advice, but Ben was younger, and hip, and cool, and Theo didn't want to look like he was trying too hard.

Was the jacket trying too hard?

Before he could decide if he should fling it off as if it were a rabid octopus and toss it in the nearest bank of shrubs, Katie broke through the crowd and caught his eye. Her face lit up, and it took her a few moments to navigate through the people on the boardwalk to arrive at his side. And she'd already seen the jacket, so he'd have to keep it for now.

"Look at you," she said, reaching out and trailing her fingers down the lapel of his jacket. She didn't even touch his body, but the strongest current of electricity zipped through him as if she'd hooked him to a live wire.

He decided to play up the casualness of his outfit, because she was wearing a pair of jean cutoffs and a tank top the color of peaches. He was starting to notice the fruit in everything about her, and he turned in a slow circle, his arms out. "You like this, don't you?"

She laughed, and it could've been the carefree laugh of the twenty-two-year-old he'd first fallen in love with. He faced her again, and she wore laughter and happiness on her face. "I can't lie. I do like this. It doesn't make sense." She scanned him from head to toe and back. "I mean, the jeans with the white stitching. You know those are totally out, right? And the T-shirt. Did you buy it that faded?" She flipped the hem of it, her fingers getting very close to skin that time.

Theo felt too hot in the jacket, even though they still stood in the shade, and he felt like a moron for spending so much on a T-shirt that was so faded. "Should we get in line?" he asked, indicating the four lines that ran up to the converted mobile home that was now a taco stand.

"Sure." She hugged herself and stepped off the wooden walkway and onto the sand. "What do you like here?" She twisted back to him. "You have eaten here, haven't you?"

"Oh, sure," he said. "I live and work just down the beach."

"Oh, yeah? Where?"

"I have a condo on the Ohana block."

"Oh, North tower or South tower?"

He stepped beside her as they joined the line. "South," he said, deciding to withhold that it faced the beach and had an entire wall of windows.

"And where's your office?"

"Um, in a condo on the Ohana block."

She scoffed, somehow turning it into a giggle. "So you work from home."

"Sort of."

She turned toward him and shaded her eyes. "Sort of?"

Theo looked at her through his sunglasses, wondering if the mirrored lenses really kept his eyes concealed. And he wanted to be honest with her, so he said, "I own two condos in the South tower, and I live in one and work out of the other."

She blinked, clearly not expecting him to say that. "You have two condos in the South tower."

"Mm-hm, that's right." He inched forward, suddenly wishing the sand would suddenly suck him down into a sinkhole.

A full minute went by before she said, "So you're rich."

That was putting it mildly, but Theo didn't need to

blurt out how many zeroes currently resided in his bank account. "I do okay," he said.

"Hey, Theo."

He turned toward the male voice and saw Jasper Rosequist stepping off the beachwalk. He looked like he belonged on the beach, complete with the windswept hair and billionaire swagger.

"Jasper." He shook the man's hand as he joined them in line. "This is Katie…." Theo's mind blanked. He couldn't just say "H." The woman had a real last name.

"Harrison," Katie said. "My last name is Harrison." She shook Jasper's hand too before giving Theo a pointed stare.

"Oh, this is Jasper Rosequist," he said. "He works with —" He cut off his voice, realizing that if he introduced his friend as a diamond mogul, then Katie would know that he did more than okay.

"Diamonds," Jasper said, giving Theo a curious look too. "I work in the diamond business."

"Oh, that's great." Katie took a step forward. "You do okay, my left foot." She elbowed him, which caused him to recoil though her touch didn't hurt. "You're rich."

"So one of my businesses finally took off," he said.

"What? Third time's the charm?" she asked as if Jasper wasn't standing right there.

Theo didn't really care. Jasper knew a lot about him anyway. He was the one who'd invited Theo to the Nine-0 Club, and then spent a lot of time chatting about the consumer market, supply and demand, and what someone might pay for a certain product or service.

"I think Software Solutions was my sixth try, actually," he said. And he didn't think it. He knew it.

Another step forward, and Katie hadn't fled yet. Now with Jasper with them, was this even a date?

"So what did you do this weekend?" he asked her, and Jasper pulled in a breath.

"Hey, I have to go," he said, bolting as fast as he'd joined them. A few seconds later, Theo's phone buzzed against his thigh, but he ignored it.

"Heather loves the beach," Katie said. "So we spent a lot of time there. And I like to garden, so she tended to her cats while I worked in the backyard."

"Her cats?" Theo wasn't exactly a feline-lover.

"Oh, we don't own any of them," Katie said, reaching back to tighten her ponytail. "She puts out food and water for the strays. I'm sure the neighbors hate us." She gave a light laugh, and Theo joined in.

"I'm sure they do." Someone edged past him with a full tray, bumping him closer to Katie. He entered her personal space, very aware of the scent of oranges and something antiseptic-like.

"Sorry," he said, not at all sorry to be this close to her. He put his hand on her waist to keep himself from tipping over, and when he could settle back onto his feet, he slipped his hand into hers.

She didn't yank her fingers away or say anything. She did tip her head back and look at him, questions swimming in her eyes. Theo had no idea how to answer them, and it was their turn to step forward and order anyway.

"What do you want?" he asked.

"What do you think I want?"

He gazed at her for a moment, wondering if he messed up if that would be it for them. This was their second date, and if he survived this, he'd be well on his way to a third —which would be the most he'd been out with the same woman in a while.

Turning back to the cashier, he said, "We'll have two orders of fish tacos."

"Guacamole?"

"Yes, on both."

"Drinks?"

"A large water bottle for me, and she'll have the peach lemonade." He pulled his wallet out of his back pocket, feeling the offensive white stitching on his jeans, and paid for their lunch. Once they had their cardboard containers of fish tacos, he said, "So why don't you tell me what you'd like in an app for Clean Sweep."

"You remember the name of my cleaning company?"

He pretended to search for a spot to sit and chin-nodded to her left. "Over there." They sat at the end of a picnic table that already had another couple at the other end, and he tried to find a reason he could remember the name of her cleaning company.

"I looked you up online."

She froze halfway through unwrapping her straw. "You did not."

"No judgment," he said. "I just wanted to see what I was working with. You think I'd come to our meeting unprepared?"

She finished unwrapping the straw and plunked it in

her lemonade, her eyes never leaving his. She possessed fire and grit, and he liked that about her. He always had. "Is that what this is? A meeting?"

"I asked you if you wanted help with an app. You said yes."

Katie ignored her food completely and leaned her elbows on the table. "Then you held my hand."

"I didn't hear any complaining." Theo wanted to suck the words back into his throat the moment he said them. "That's not what…." He sighed. "Look, I'll just say it. I haven't been on a third date with a woman in a long time, and I'd really like to get there with you."

"You told me that already," she said, finally training those captivating eyes somewhere but on him. "And if this is a meeting, then you're still at one with me."

"Fine," he said, not wanting to talk about it anymore. He'd much prefer the technical talk of what she wanted for her app. "I assume you came prepared for the meeting too."

"Why would you assume that?"

"Because I know you." Theo looked up from his tacos, surprise coursing through him. Their eyes met, and that tether that had always bound them to each other connected and tightened.

She swiped over the screen of her phone and said, "I may have made a few notes."

He chuckled and took a big bite, remembering that he'd also gotten a text while standing in line. He pulled out his phone and checked it to see Jasper's name. *You're on a date! I'm so sorry. Talk later.*

Theo navigated away from the text quickly and went to his app store. He could talk features for hours, and he told himself he'd only allow a few minutes. Let her ask her questions and go over her notes.

"So I'm wondering if there's a way I can communicate with my maids," she said. "And the customer can too, and they can see it all on the back end."

"Of course," he said. "That's a more sophisticated app, but definitely something we can do for you."

She nodded slowly as she chewed, and he showed her an app he'd developed for a client that did similar things to what she wanted. It was for a plumbing business, but the customer side showed people which times and dates were available, and they scheduled.

On the backside, all the plumbers attached to the app could see the request come in and one of them would take it and add it to their schedule. "And the boss—that would be you—can communicate with them too, with things like messages, calendar items, even setting meeting times and attaching files."

She'd finished her tacos several minutes ago, but Theo still had two of his. He pushed the button to turn off his phone and he picked up his food. "Questions? You look…." Something. He wasn't sure if she was worried or upset or what.

"I don't think I can afford an app like that."

"I can redo your website too. Integrate it." He took a huge bite of his now cold tacos. Didn't matter. The mango salsa was still fruity and spicy, and the fish flaky and delicious.

"My website really is a mess, isn't it?"

He shook his head as he finished chewing and swallowing. "I'd actually call it a disaster." He chuckled, glad when her laughter joined in with his. "I wasn't even sure where to go. But we can fix all of that. And requests that come through the website will sync with the app. You seem good with the technology, and there's no reason not to use it."

"Except the price tag. You've never said how much this all costs."

Theo studied her, trying to find the right words. The ones that wouldn't drive her away, that wouldn't freak her out.

He came up with, "This one's on me."

She shook her head, the high ponytail swinging violently. "Oh, no. That's not happening."

"Fine." Theo should've known she wouldn't take charity. She'd never been particularly good at letting someone help her. It probably made her a great single mom. "The integrated service is one dollar."

She scoffed. "I'm calling your office for a quote."

"Go right ahead."

As she swiped to find the number, he sent a quick text to Ben.

She lifted the phone to her ear, a triumphant look on her face. "Yes, hello. I'm just wondering if you can give me a quote real quick? Great....yes, I'd like a website remake, and something that integrates into the app."

Her eyes would not let go of his, and Theo was

enjoying himself entirely too much. She said, "Yes...no... business applications, yes...backend, huh? Yes, that too."

He smiled at her, and she looked away. But her almost shrieked, "One dollar?" brought her attention back to him.

He shrugged and stacked their garbage to take it to the trashcan. When he returned to the table, she said, "You're a sneaky one, Theo. I was not expecting that."

Theo slung his arm around her shoulders. "Let me do this for you." He didn't mean for his voice to come out with quite so much tenderness and emotion in it. Surely Katie heard it.

He definitely heard her when she said, "Okay," and his heart grew wings and began to flap around excitedly in his chest.

They parted on the beachwalk, her heading west while he went east back to his condo, without a plan for their next date. But no matter what, he'd be seeing her again, and that knowledge propelled him back to the office.

"Now," he said as he sat down at his command center —three monitors on his L-shaped desk. "I just need to know *why* she let me help her."

Because if there was one thing Katie was and always had been, it was fiercely independent. So what was really going on with the owner of the seemingly successful Clean Sweep?

Theo intended to find out on their next date.

FIVE

KATIE WAITED in the driveway of Gertrude Chu, her annoyance rising with every passing minute. Mrs. Chu was constantly running late, and she wouldn't allow Katie into the house to clean without her there.

But Katie didn't have time to waste today. She'd called Mrs. Chu and been assured in broken English that the older woman was on her way home. Twenty minutes had passed, and Katie didn't know anywhere on the island that took that long to get to, besides the cattle ranch way out on the western curve. And surely Mrs. Chu wouldn't have business out there.

Yet she hadn't arrived at home yet. Katie's patience dwindled to almost nothing, and she sent a text to her next client to explain she'd be a little late. The ripple effects from losing a half an hour waiting on a job were disastrous. She'd be later picking Heather up from the after-school club she attended, which meant she'd have to pay an additional fee.

Dinner would be later. Katie would be more irritable.

All because a woman didn't trust Katie with a key or a garage code. Finally, just when Katie was about to call Mrs. Chu and reschedule, the woman pulled into her driveway.

Katie got out and collected her huge bucket of cleaning supplies. She gave Mrs. Chu a look when they met in the garage. "I've been waiting for almost forty minutes, Mrs. Chu," she said. "It really would be easier if you gave me a key." She spoke in a professional and kind manner, which was the exact opposite of how she felt.

"Sorry, sorry," Mrs. Chu said, bustling up the few steps and into the house. She held the door for Katie, who put on her strongest work ethic and busted through the chores at Mrs. Chu's house.

If she could, she'd give Mrs. Chu to someone else, but the woman wouldn't allow that either. She bowed Katie out of the house with cash in her hand, and Katie drove ten over the speed limit to her next client's house.

Avery Lind just wanted her bathrooms cleaned and every floor in the house done. Once a month, Katie did a deep-cleaning job like scrubbing the refrigerator from top to bottom or wiping down all the cupboards. But today, she mopped and vacuumed, wiped and polished, before hurrying to the after-care club to pick up Heather.

"Sorry," she said as she entered the large multi-purpose room where Heather sat at a table alone, her head bent over something as she worked.

"It's fine," Tina said, picking up her own purse. Of

course it wasn't okay. Katie had delayed Tina from going home too.

She flashed a smile and headed over to the table. Sitting, she groaned, sighed, and said, "What are you painting?"

"The mountains," Heather said, her brush moving in swift strokes across the paper.

Katie wondered where she'd ever seen mountains. They certainly didn't have any in Kansas, and while Hawaii was an island chain of the tops of mountains, they weren't like the Rockies or anything.

Tina sat down across from Heather. "Are you going to tell your mom what we talked about?"

Heather met Tina's eye, a bit nervous. But Tina smiled, her teeth bright and white against her darker skin. So nothing serious.

"Oh, yeah." Heather put her brush down in the tray and twisted to face Katie. "Miss Tina says I should enter the community art contest." Her dark eyes held excitement and hope, and Katie couldn't remember the last time she felt like that about anything. Maybe when she and Claire had started Clean Sweep.

"Oh? When is that?" Katie asked, looking at the mountains again. She could barely tell what it was, and she wondered what Tina saw that Katie couldn't.

"It's always held in December," Tina said. "As part of the Christmas festival." She picked up Heather's tray of paints. "She's quite talented."

"I thought you were going to bake for the festival this

year," Katie said as Tina walked away and started cleaning up the tray of paint in the sink.

"I am," Heather said. "I have time to do both. I'm here every day anyway, and I don't like the sports. Miss Tina said I can stay in with her and paint if I have a project."

So perhaps Tina had offered the idea out of pity. The idea didn't sit well with Katie, but she didn't want to be the one to douse her daughter's hope with cold water. She was only ten. Life would certainly have plenty of ice water to throw on her dreams.

Bitterness crept up Katie's throat, but she swallowed it back and smiled. "Sure. It's a great idea." She stood, her muscles protesting mightily at the movement. She knew better than to sit down before she was done working for the day, and she was most certainly not finished with everything yet that day. "Come on, bug. We need to get home and get dinner going."

Heather stood up and shouldered her backpack. They left with Tina, who said she'd get an entrance form for Heather, and once they were in the car, Katie said, "How about we pick something up for dinner tonight? I don't feel like cooking."

Usually when Katie suggested that, Heather would volunteer to make something easy like grilled cheese sandwiches or spaghetti. But tonight, she said, "Me either," and looked out the passenger window with a sigh.

"You okay?" Katie asked, her mind flipping through places she could go for dinner. There were dozens of fast food or fast casual places, but some of them didn't have drive-throughs, and she honestly wasn't sure she could get out of the car and go into another building that wasn't her house.

"Why were you late tonight?"

"Mrs. Chu," Katie said, an inkling of darkness entering her voice. She reached over and patted Heather's leg. "You know I'd be home with you all the time if I could, right?"

Heather swung her head toward Katie, her dark eyes round and watery now. "I know." Her voice sounded tinny, and Katie waited for the tears to come. At first, she'd been concerned when her seemingly normal and well-adjusted daughter randomly cried, claiming she wasn't sure why she was sad. Only that she was.

Over the last three years since it had started, Katie let her cry, usually as they laid together in Heather's bed, and she stroked her hair, and sang her nursery rhymes from her babyhood.

"Have you heard from Dad?" Heather asked as the first of the tears splashed her cheeks.

"Of course I haven't," Katie said in a quiet voice. "I tell you every time I do." Her second ex-husband got to email sometimes, and he'd sent a birthday card for Heather every year despite his incarceration.

"Someone at school today said I couldn't come to their birthday party because I didn't have a dad."

"What does that have to do with anything?" Katie asked, instantly hot and furious. The reason Ray was in jail was *not* her fault. And yet she felt like she and Heather paid the price of his decisions every single day of their lives.

"I guess it's a daddy-daughter party." Heather sniffled,

this episode much shorter and less intense than others had been.

Katie bit back the words, "You wouldn't want him there anyway." Heather had been too young to understand what was really going on with her dad. She knew he was there one day and gone the next. Living in Kansas for kindergarten and then moving to Hawaii, where they'd lived ever since.

They'd had many talks since then, but her memories of Ray were childlike at best, and Katie actually wanted to keep it that way.

"I find it hard to believe you're the only one without a dad," she said. "And you have a dad. He's just not here with us."

"And he never will be," Heather said, a hint of bitterness in her tone.

Katie pressed her lips together. "No, Heather, he never will be." She thought of Theo, but immediately dismissed the thought. However, maybe Heather could take another man and go to the party. Katie knew plenty of men.

"Could you go if you had a man with you?"

"I don't know." Heather turned back to the window. "I don't care anyway."

But it was obvious that she did.

"Whose party is it?"

"Amelia Grace."

Katie almost winced but managed to turn the motion into her moving to turn on the blinker so they could turn onto their street. "I'll call her mom tonight and ask."

"Who would I go with?"

"I don't know," Katie said. "Claire's boyfriend?" She glanced at Heather, but she wasn't looking at Katie. "You like Chuck, right?"

"Yeah, he's nice."

Katie patted her daughter's knee and turned into their driveway. It wasn't until she put the car in park that she realized she'd never stopped to get dinner.

"It's fine," Heather said when Katie lamented their lack of readily available food. "I'll throw in a frozen pizza while you check all the timecards."

———

"So what did Chuck say?" Theo asked, watching Katie lift her steaming cup of coffee to her lips.

"Oh, he can go." She sipped, very aware of the way Theo's eyes tracked every movement she made. She half liked it and half wished he'd take the staring down a notch. "Heather was very happy about it."

Theo had been a great listener at their quick get-together for coffee. Though it was still plenty warm, Katie liked nothing better than a good cup of coffee, with flavored creams and fancy big-chunk sugars.

He'd been messaging her for a week now, and she couldn't put him off any longer. Didn't want to put him off at all. But she also didn't want to come across as desperate to see him again.

So when she'd suggested that she had forty-five minutes for coffee, he'd said he'd meet her in the new Brew Bar on the ground floor of the Sweet Breeze Resort and Spa. He'd even beat her there, which surprised her as her office was only a block away and she'd come straight over.

They'd only talked about Heather today, all mentions of her website or app staying silent. She met his eye, realizing he'd asked her something and she'd missed it. "I'm sorry, what?"

He shook his head, a smile touching that powerful mouth and making her warmer than she thought possible. "I just said she's lucky to have a mom like you."

"Hmm," she said. She was actually surprised Theo hadn't asked why Heather's father wasn't in Getaway Bay with them, but perhaps he was biding his time. Waiting for a better opportunity.

Her phone bleeped and his did too, almost in tandem. "Oh, wow," she said, picking up her device. It had given her and Theo another date recommendation. "Parasailing?" She looked at him, her eyebrows lifted as if they were asking him if he'd go with her.

"I got the same thing," he said, setting his phone face down on the table.

"Should we go?"

Those bright blue eyes came back to hers. "You want to go parasailing with me?"

Katie was quite tired, and she was much too old to play games. She'd avoided him for eight days before suggesting coffee. He was handsome in his light gray suit, the black striped tie knotted just-so at his throat. She let her eyes fall to that knot, wondering what it would take to get him to loosen up around her.

Or maybe this was the loose version of Theo, especially now that he clearly had more money than a person would ever need.

"Yes." She looked back at him, almost daring him to turn her down. "Theo, will you go out with me?"

"Of course," he said, his voice catching on the very last syllable. He cleared his throat, and she couldn't be sure, but she thought she saw a hint of a flush stain his neck. He signaled the waiter that they were ready to pay, and he put a fifty-dollar bill on the tray before claiming her hand and saying, "Do you have time for to walk me back to my office?"

Katie didn't really have time to do that, no, but the feel of her hand in his was too delicious to pass up. They strolled along the beachwalk, and he told her about Ben, a man who worked with him in the condo-slash-office.

"That's all you've got?" she asked. "One man?"

"Here," he said. "My company runs out of Dallas. I've got oh, probably four hundred employees there."

And Katie thought she'd been doing well to have seventeen. *You are,* she told herself. All of her girls worked every day, so she had a lot of clients.

Theo stopped at The Straw and bought her a Peach Power smoothie before sweeping his lips across her forehead and saying, "I can tell I'm boring you. Thanks for the coffee. I'll call you later."

He left her standing in the shade outside the smoothie stand, waiting for them to call her name, the burning, tingling, absolutely electrifying sensation of his lips on her skin pounding through her bloodstream.

"How's he going to call me?" she whispered to the trees and sand. After all, he didn't have her phone number, as all of their communication had been through the app.

She yanked her phone out of her pocket and typed quickly. *You weren't boring me. And if you really want to call, here's my number.*

"Katie," a woman called, and she jumped, accidentally adding two extra sixes on the end of the number. She strode forward and got her peach smoothie, erased the extra numbers, and hit send before she could question every decision she'd made in the past forty-six years.

SIX

"ARE you sure you want to do this?" Theo eyed the boat, all the wires and ropes, and that huge reel on the back of it with suspicion.

Katie tightened the strap on her helmet and picked up the bag the instructor had given her. "What? You don't?"

No, he didn't want to fling himself off the back of a speed boat and hope his parachute deployed. He valued his life, thank you very much. And he most certainly didn't remember Katie as a thrill seeker.

"Of course I want to," he lied, hoping the little white fib wouldn't blossom into something he couldn't control. "I'm just surprised you do."

"Have you been on the monster zipline yet?" She stepped onto the boat like she did it every day of her life.

"Monster zipline?" Theo stared at her, very hesitant to leave dry land. Yes, he'd been through the orientation.

Intellectually, he knew what to do. The videos did look fun. But actually doing it?

She laughed. "Yeah, it's the longest zipline in the United States. It's beautiful, out over the forests over on the cattle ranch side of the island." She cocked her hip and put one hand on it. "You don't want to do this."

"Not especially, no," he said. And he couldn't believe she did anything with the word "monster" in the title. Twenty years ago, she wouldn't even allow zombie movies in the house.

"But GBS recommended it," she said with a teasing quality in her voice. "Why would they do that if you hadn't fed them something to indicate you liked this kind of activity?" She giggled, and Theo definitely wanted her to keep doing that. "Hmm?"

"There's something I should probably tell you," he said, stepping onto the boat. It didn't rock like mad and spit him into the ocean, and his nerves went down a rung.

"What's that?"

"Apps are just machines," he said. "Not everything GBS says and recommends is one-hundred percent accurate."

"But it's our roadmap to a great relationship," she said.

Theo cringed at the tagline, hearing the accompanying jingle in his head. "Yes, but...I just don't think it's always right."

"What makes you say that?" She watched him with curiosity in her expression, her head cocked slightly to the side, probably thinking he'd had some disastrous dating experiences to speak of.

He wished he did, because if he told her, she'd become the fifth person on the Earth to know how he'd earned his billions.

"Because I invented it," he said. He knew every line of code, every parenthesis and every parameter. And it was a machine, and it could fail, make mistakes, and was only as good as the information fed into it.

"You two ready?" The instructor practically dive-bombed onto the boat, jostling Theo and making him throw his hands out to latch onto something. That something, unfortunately, was Katie, and she sucked in a breath as he curled his fingers around her bare upper arm.

Then her pealing laughter filled the sky, and pure humiliation filled Theo from top to bottom.

"You've got the helmets and bags," the instructor said. Theo strained to remember the man's name, thinking it was something like Ed or Al or something short. "So all you need are life jackets."

He grinned like the Cheshire Cat, and Theo didn't feel comforted from the width of it. He took the life jacket, though, and stuffed his arms through the holes, tightening it almost to the point of painful.

"Your helmet," Katie said, extending it toward him with an equally maniacal smile on her face. "This is going to be so fun."

"Have you done this before?" Ed/Al asked, and she said, "No, but I've always wanted to."

He stood behind the steering wheel and gave no warning when he accelerated. Theo almost went toppling into the reel on the back of the boat, and he cursed silently.

Cursed his app that had recommended this date. Cursed the coupon emails that Katie received which had advertised the very parasailing she wanted to do.

She'd bought their tickets and then called him. "Saturday," she'd said. "Tell me you're not busy about noon."

"No," he'd said before realizing what he was committing to. And honestly, at the time, he didn't care. If she wanted to drive up to the dormant volcano and sacrifice him on Saturday at noon, he probably would've agreed to it. He just wanted to keep seeing her, keep talking to her, keep learning more and more about her.

Which was why he braced himself as Ed/Al accelerated again, a whoop coming from his mouth that did little to inspire confidence in Theo that his parasailing instructor was actually a responsible, careful man.

Sure enough, he took them out into the ocean until there were no other boats nearby. Wasn't there some sort of buddy system for boats? If so, this guy had just broken it.

He gave a few more instructions, and then he had Katie come over and get strapped into all the wires and ropes and cords and who knows what else.

"You guys will be tandem sailing," he said. "One off each side."

"Won't we run into each other?" Theo didn't even like to swing next to someone, worried about twisting and turning and crashing and burning.

"Nah," Ed/Al said.

"Have people ever hit each other?" Theo asked next, wondering why these weren't on the FAQ portion of the Bonnet Yacht Club's website.

"Not that I'm aware of." The instructor gave Theo a wary glance. "You'll be fine, man. You ready?"

Theo was not ready, nor was he fine, but he allowed Ed/Al to strap him in and tell him to perch on the very small corner of the boat, where two yellow feet had been painted. He resumed his position at the steering wheel, but instead of blasting off and throwing Theo backward into the water, he operated a hydraulic winch, moving it over toward Katie first. She sat; he buckled; Theo watched.

"Your turn," he said, and Theo took the seat beside Katie, a feeling a complete serenity washing over him.

Once everything was ready, he said, "Okay, you've got the eight-hundred-foot line, which is as high as the FAA allows us to go." He grinned. "It's going to be great."

Theo braced himself, wishing there was more to hold onto than the straps connected to the bar above him. But he gripped them like his life depended on it, expecting the worst.

Katie didn't even hold on to anything, and when the lift started and they rose effortlessly, without a single bump, foolishness raced through Theo. Then pure exhilaration and joy. He laughed as the boat got smaller and the view larger. "This is amazing," he said, his breath actually catching in his throat. The wide expanse of water before him stole his breath, as did the woman at his side.

He reached over and took her hand in his. "I was wrong. GBS was totally right and didn't lead me astray."

She beamed at him, the wind pushing her hair back. "So you invented GBS, huh? No wonder you're rich."

"Well." He shrugged, though he knew he was rich. It

was everything he'd ever wanted—the money. But the fame? He could do without that.

"Tell me about that," she said.

"About GBS?"

"Yeah."

"I'd been working on a piece of dating software for a while," he said. "But I wanted something interactive, and our social media accounts are able to take our behaviors and produce ads that they think will entice us to buy. So I took that concept and put it in the relationship arena. It's done well here, and we've expanded to over two hundred urban markets now."

"Wow."

Wow was right, but Theo didn't say it. "I came here, because…I'd heard of something I wanted to learn more about. And when I got here and couldn't get a date, we launched GBS."

"But the app's been around for at least a couple of years. You haven't." She looked at him, wiping her hair off her face. "Have you?"

"No, I moved here permanently just last year," he said. "But I'd visited the island quite a lot before then."

She squeezed his hand and pointed to her left. He leaned forward, sure shifting the balance would throw them off, but nothing happened. The huge smiley face parachute behind them adjusted, and he saw splashing below.

"Dolphins?" he asked.

"I'm sure." She turned to him, a huge smile on her face, and Theo had never been happier than he'd created

Getaway Bay Singles—and not just for the money this time. But because the app had allowed him to reconnect with someone he'd never stopped loving.

———

The following Wednesday started like any other. Theo ran on the treadmill in the spare bedroom of his condo. He ate two eggs for breakfast, with a fruit cup full of red grapefruit. He took his coffee black and headed downstairs to the office.

He arrived before Ben, as usual, and stood overlooking the beach while he sipped his caffeine for the day. With his adrenaline humming, he sat in front of the computer to check email and take care of menial things before diving into his projects.

He'd been working on the same two for so long, he almost wanted to can them, burn the files, and start over with different prospects.

But if he could just get Island Airways to sign with him to build the app and website, it wouldn't matter if he lost every other client tomorrow. They were the white whale, the one client he needed to keep all others afloat.

He'd been talking with their tech department, the CEO, and their chief engineers for ten months. Ten long months. Meetings. Lunches. Drinks. And he felt ready to either throw in the towel or get something inked.

He'd also spoken one more time to Lawrence Gladstone at the last Nine-0 Club meeting, and he just needed signatures on the Gladstone Financial paperwork. Ben had finalized it all yesterday, and Lawrence was supposed to be dropping by that morning.

Thus, the little things had to be done so Theo could focus on the bigger rocks.

So he sipped, and he checked, and he answered. Just as he pulled the Island Airlines file toward him, another email came in.

His heart raced, and he couldn't seem to read fast enough. But Alexander Mitchell had emailed, and Theo fumbled as he tried to align his hand on the mouse. He finally clicked open the email from the CEO of Island Airlines to see the words *We're ready to go over final paperwork and sign. When's a good time for you to meet?*

Theo started laughing, and laughing, and laughing.

Ben found him, still cackling in front of the computer. "What is going on?" he asked, setting a paper bag on Theo's desk. "I could hear you as soon as I got off the elevator."

"Alex is ready to sign." Theo looked up, the blank email response still waiting for him to type something into it.

"Alex Mitchell?" Ben darted around the desk and into Theo's cave of screens. "You're kidding."

"I'm not kidding." Theo stood up and grabbed Ben in a bear hug. "We did it! We got the biggest commercial airline out of Hawaii to take on our app." He clapped Ben on the back and released him, more emotions than he knew what to do with streaming through him. "Help me formulate a response."

"He wants to know when we can meet." Ben pulled out his phone. "I'm getting your calendar now."

"We both need to be there." Theo reached for the bag and hoped there were pastries inside. Of course there were, from the best doughnut shop on the island: Nuts About Dough.

"Today we have Lawrence coming in before noon. I have a phone call with Talbots this afternoon that I can reschedule. When is he thinking? Today?"

"I have no idea." Theo abandoned the email and dialed Alex instead. "Hey," he said when the CEO himself answered. "I just got your email and thought maybe a chat would get us to a meeting sooner. I'm going to put you on speaker, okay?"

"That's fine," Alex said, his big, bold voice practically deafening Theo. "Let me go out with Sandra. Then she can pull up my calendar too."

They spoke back and forth for a few minutes, each vetoing days or times until finally, next Tuesday at one o'clock, they could meet. Ben and Theo would go to the Island Airways corporate offices near the airport, and everything would be signed, sealed, and app development would begin.

When Theo hung up, he sat back in his seat, utterly stunned. "I can't believe it," he said.

Ben chuckled, pulled out a doughnut, and checked his phone when it sounded at him. "Oh, Lawrence is here."

"Two huge new accounts," he said. And huge was an understatement. His euphoria died a little, because he knew he'd be hands-on for these two specific clients. He'd be building their apps, running the meetings, making the phone calls, doing the testing.

And that meant he wouldn't have nearly as much time to dedicate to the messaging he'd been doing on GBS with a certain brown-haired beauty he wanted to make a more permanent part of his life.

It'll be fine, he told himself. Katie knew what he did for a living. She worked long hours too. "It will all be fine."

SEVEN

"OH, NO," Katie groaned, her attention on her phone. With her hair still damp and framing her face in curls, she collapsed onto the bed. Another week had gone by since the most romantic parasailing she'd ever done.

Fine, it had been the only time she'd been parasailing, but holding Theo's hand and talking about business, life, and cats had been one of the best hours of her life.

She stared at the texts from Chuck, sure the letters had arranged themselves into the wrong order. He *had* to go to the party with Heather that evening. He just *had* to.

But all of his messages said he couldn't. Something at work had come up, and since he was a paramedic, when duty called, he had to answer it.

She let her phone fall to her lap, searching for another solution.

"Hey, Mom." Heather skipped into the room and sat on

the bed beside her, sobering immediately. "What's wrong?"

Katie pressed her lips together. She couldn't tell her. She just couldn't. She'd worked hard to give Heather a stress-free life, somewhere soft to fall, somewhere easy to learn life's disappointments. But she tried to shelter her from as much as possible.

"Mom, what's going on?"

Katie held out her phone and Heather took it. "Oh, no," she said, and Katie heard herself in her daughter's voice. "Well, I guess that's it." She stood and handed the phone back to Katie.

"I have another idea," Katie said, feeling irrational and insane. Theo would definitely say no. Should she get Heather's hopes up for nothing?

"Who?" Heather asked.

"Let me talk to him first," she said. "I don't want to promise you anything."

"Who is it? Do I even know him?"

"Sort of."

"Sort of?"

"Go get the white album," Katie said. "And I'll call him."

Heather gave her one more doubt-filled look, then turned and left the bedroom. Katie hurried after her, closing the door and locking it so her daughter couldn't come in during the conversation.

She lost her confidence and decided to message him through GBS first. *Hey, so I have a huge favor to ask. Remember how I told you about Heather and that daddy-*

daughter birthday party? Well, Chuck can't go...and I wondered if you would take Heather.

Her finger stalled over the send arrow as desperation clawed its way through her. She didn't want to proofread or make things sound better than they were. She quickly hit send and then added, *It's a birthday party for the most popular girl in fifth grade, and it'll likely be a nightmare. But Heather really wants to go. I will buy you dinner for a year if you go.*

She'd barely hit send when she got a message back from Theo. *What time?*

Was he truly considering it?

5:00.

I can go. And you don't need to buy me dinner. I would, however, like to go on the monster zipline with you. Can we make that happen?

Relief rushed through Katie so strongly that tears pricked her eyes. Her chest heaved with a single sob, and then she shoved her motherly emotions away. *We can definitely make the monster zipline happen,* she typed out and sent before launching to her feet and opening the door.

Heather sat on the other side of the hall, her knees up in front of her and the white picture album hugged to her chest. "Come on in," Katie said. "And I'll show you who you're going to the party with."

"He said yes?" Heather scrambled to her feet, her face alight with such hope that Katie's chest pinched.

"He indeed said yes." She took the book from her daughter and led her to the bed. "Now, his name is Theo. He's the man I've been out with a few times over the past month." She flipped open the book, noting that the pictures were faded and well-loved. She'd told Heather all about the photographs in this book, some more detailed than others.

Near the end, a single photo of her and Theo remained from their time as husband and wife. She pointed to him. "That's him. Theo Fleming. He's got gray hair now."

"He's old?"

"Only a couple of years older than me," her mom said. "Just the same age as all of your friends' dads, I promise." He grinned out at her from the pictures, his face so handsome. Katie hadn't realized how much she'd missed him until that moment.

"Is that you?" Heather asked, leaning forward.

"Yes," Katie said slowly. "Heather, Theo and I were married once."

Heather lifted her eyes from the album to meet her mom's. "What? You were married before Dad?"

"Yes."

"To Theo."

"Yes." Katie watched as the wheels began turning in her daughter's head. She focused on something else, her mouth hanging open.

"I like him," Katie whispered. "And he'll be here at four-forty to take you to the party, so you better be ready."

She cleared her throat, unsure if she'd spoken the first few words out loud or not. Heather pushed herself off the bed and said, "I have to wrap the present first," as if she didn't still have hours before the shindig began.

She left the room, left Katie to her own thoughts. *I like him.*

She wasn't lying, and she felt Theo burrow his way into the softer, fleshier part of her heart once again.

"Hola," Claire called, and Katie slapped the white photo album closed and shoved it under the comforter before her best friend could pop her head into the bedroom. "There you are."

"Here I am." Katie put on the best smile she could muster, knowing she'd tell Claire everything in under five minutes.

"What's going on?" Claire asked in a warning tone as she entered the bedroom. "Chuck says he's so, so sorry. But apparently the quarterback got himself stuck out on some tropical island, and everyone's been called in."

"Maine Fitzgerald?"

"The one and only. His coaches called him in missing a couple of days ago. Everyone thought he was just blowing off steam or something." She sat on the bed next to Katie— and jumped right back up. "Ow. What's under there?"

With a great big sigh, Katie heaved out the photo album.

"Oh, honey." Claire took the book. "Going through old times again?"

"Kind of," Katie said. "When Chuck cancelled, I decided to call Theo."

"Ooh, The-o," Claire sang. "And?"

"And he said yes, so I was just showing him to Heather. That's all." But it so wasn't all, and if Claire believed Katie when she spoke in such a false tone, it would be a miracle.

Claire snorted and said, "Yeah, right." She flipped open the book and leafed aimlessly through the pages. "Just admit it. You like him."

Katie shrugged, not committing to anything quite yet. But she'd enjoyed every meeting with him, every cup of coffee, every parasailing adventure. A smile touched her mouth, and Claire said, "I know that look. You really like him."

Katie did, but a fair amount of frustration built up inside her too. "He's just so easy, you know?" She looked at Claire, desperate for validation. "Like, I was married to the guy." She stood up and ran her hands down her arms, hugging herself tight. "He's so familiar, and yet so…new, too."

"Shiny and new," Claire said, closing the book. "Like a nickel. Silver, and strong, and gorgeous…." She laughed as she handed the album to Katie and passed her on her way out of the room. "I better get to work. And you better get figuring out how to keep Mister Tall, Dreamy, and Delicious this time."

Katie let her go, trying to sort through her feelings. One thing was for sure—she hadn't had to fight to keep Theo last time. *She'd* been the one to leave. He'd even asked her not to go…. So maybe she needed to figure out how to *stay* with Theo this time.

———

"So how rich are we talking?" Katie asked, her eyes fixed on the locked bedroom door. Theo had called about twenty minutes ago, and she felt like a rebellious teenager, taking up too much time on the landline as she talked to her boyfriend.

He'd called to get more specifics on the party, and she'd mentioned something about Amelia Grace's family being quite wealthy. He'd said, "I'm sure I can handle them," things had snowballed from there.

He'd said he'd invented the smart dating app, and it was now in production in over two hundred urban markets. That was some serious cash. Millions. Maybe even billions.

Her head swam at the thought of all that money, and she wasn't sure why. She'd never been fascinated with the dollar, not the way Theo had been. He'd wanted to be a billionaire for as long as she'd known him—in fact, it was his goal to do so by age thirty. She'd left him, broke and penniless, at age twenty-nine, so unless he had a major turn-around in the subsequent twelve months, she didn't think he'd achieved that particular goal.

But Katie knew better than most that goals morphed and changed. They were liquid, easily transforming when they needed to.

"I don't want to tell you," he said.

"So I'll guess." She lay on her back, relaxing now that she knew Heather probably wouldn't come beating down the door. And Claire had left an hour ago. "Millionaire?"

"Far exceeded," he said.

"Billionaire?"

"Mm."

She sat up, excitement pouring through her. "Congratulations, Theo," she said, and she meant it. "I know you've always wanted that title."

"It came a bit on the belated side," he said. "But I have always wanted it."

"And you semi-retired to Hawaii."

He chuckled. "Kind of. I still work a full-time job, which is another thing I think we need to talk about...."

"Oh, boy," she said. "Gonna start standing me up because you have to work?" She'd been teasing, but the silence coming through the other end of the line testified that she was right.

"Oh," she said.

"I signed two huge clients in the past week," he said. "Well, one on Wednesday, and one will be official in a couple more days, but they're *huge*, Katie."

"How huge?"

"Airline huge," he said. "That's going to be months of work just for the app. And I signed the biggest financial institution in the US. The owner and CEO lives here in Getaway Bay, and he's ready for a new banking app that has back-end features for employees, like we talked about with your app."

"Right, I got it." She could hear between the syllables. He really wouldn't have time for her. And maybe— "Can you still do my app?" she asked.

"Of course," he said. "We'll be in pre-development for at least a couple of months with both clients. I'm just...I guess I just...." But he trailed off and didn't say anything more.

"What, Theo?" she asked, usually not one to press a

conversation into a direction it didn't naturally go. But this felt important.

"I'll just say it, and you can tell me I'm stupid."

"If I must."

"The money doesn't matter to you, does it?" He paused, but not nearly long enough for her to breathe and answer. "It's just, I didn't think it mattered to you. Twenty years ago, you told me over and over that you didn't care how much money we had. That you just wanted to be with me." He coughed. Or maybe it was a scoff. Something.

Katie blinked, surprise darting through her. "Theo, money has never mattered all that much to me."

"Okay, good."

"It does seem like you might not have time to spend on me right now, though," she said. "I get it if you need to push my stuff back. I'm not a paying customer."

"I'm not worried about that," he said.

"All right. Well, you let me know."

"I will. Hey, I was, uh, thinking, maybe I'd bring over a treat or something, get to know Heather a little before the party." He sounded hopeful and scared at the same time, and Katie sat upright on her bed.

"When?"

"I don't know, like twenty minutes or so?"

"Twenty minutes," squeaked out of her mouth. Could she get herself presentable in twenty minutes? At least the house was already clean. "Sure."

"Great, see you then." He hung up, and Katie collapsed back onto the pillows, a warm glow emanating from her body. Theo was coming over.

And while he'd said that his two new, huge clients meant he wouldn't have time to work on her app, what she was really worried about was that he wouldn't have time to spend with her.

"But he's coming over," she said. "And bringing a treat. So he has time."

But for how long?

She couldn't brush away the thought as she swiped mascara on her eyelashes and swept pink gloss on her lips. And then he rang the doorbell, and every cell in her body rioted.

One step at a time, she told herself as she went to answer the door. That was what she'd done when she'd filed for divorce the first time. What she'd done when she found out about Ray's drug problem. What she'd done when she'd uprooted her whole life and moved with her daughter across the ocean to a new state, for a fresh start.

She could do it with Theo too.

EIGHT

THEO KNOCKED on Katie's door, already having rung the doorbell with no success. He carried a box of muffins, desperately hoping they counted as a treat.

A moment later, the door opened and Katie stood there, looking positively radiant. She leaned into the doorway. "Hey."

Theo hadn't been out of the dating pool for so long that he didn't recognize flirting when he saw it. "Hey, yourself." She seemed relaxed, but he felt like he'd swallowed a hand grenade that could explode at any moment.

"My doorbell works," she said, falling back a step to give him room to enter.

"Oh, I... thought maybe you hadn't heard me." Theo stepped into her house, the scent of the Hawaiian breeze overly tropical and barely covering the antiseptic smell of air freshener. The floors gleamed, and nothing seemed to be even a hair out of place.

"What's in the box?" she asked, leading him down a hallway and into a big open room at the back that was the kitchen, dining room, and living room.

"Muffins," he said, detouring over to the kitchen counter. No dishes in the sink. Everything was scrubbed and sanitary. He wondered if she lived like this all the time, or if she'd gone into Tasmanian devil mode and cleaned up after he'd called.

When they were married, she did clean up after meals and put things away from time to time. But it wasn't an obsession. She wasn't overly neat, nor was she messy.

"Is Heather here?" he asked, turning away from his assessment of her tidiness.

"She's finishing up a couple of things." Katie smiled at him, and he approached the couch where she sat slowly.

"Great," he said. "Do you want to talk about your app?"

"Sure."

"So I've done a thorough assessment of your website, and I think you should follow these steps." He launched into his standard speech about putting customer testimonials on the front page, with pictures of her—her, not a model—and her staff. Smiling, happy pictures with flowers and all the cleaning supplies.

"Your prices are way off," he said next. "You can be charging fifteen percent more here, and people would pay it." He glanced up, but Katie wasn't smiling and nodding along. She wore a frown and looked puzzled.

Theo continued anyway, sure her daughter was about

to burst into the room and interrupt. "And the app can match. Same pictures. I'm thinking something green. Tropical. That does really well here in Getaway Bay, and you use those Earth-friendly products—at least that's what your website says." He looked at her fully now. "Are you still using those?"

"Yes."

"And the first thing customers see when they open your app is how to book. What they can schedule and when. I think you'll see an increase of at least ten percent when we get this all up and running."

He paused, mostly because he felt out of breath. He didn't need to give the whole spiel like it was a sprint.

"I'm not raising my prices," Katie said darkly, and he clued in to the angry edge in her eyes. "I built this company on fair prices, and I'm not raising them now."

"But you could—"

"I know what I could be doing," she said, pushing herself to a standing position. "I know my website needs work, and if you think we should do green, great." She moved over to the mouth of another hallway that branched off the main one. "Heather! Theo's here. Please come out and meet him."

She turned back to him and folded her arms, clearly upset with him. "You know, it's a miracle I started a business without you. Oh, and managed to *stay* in business all these years. In fact, I wonder how I've even *survived* for the past twenty." Her eyes flashed with fire, and not the good kind that said she wanted to kiss him later.

"Katie, I—" But he had no idea what to say. And then a girl that stood almost as tall as Katie appeared at her side. Same brown hair, not too blonde, and not too dark. Same round face shape; same sloped nose.

"Yeah, Mom?"

Katie nodded toward Theo, who hastened to stand. "Theo's taking you to the birthday party. Go say hello."

Heather looked at him, a smile blooming on her face. She walked forward and extended her hand for him to shake. "Hello. I'm Heather."

He took her hand and shook it, thinking her very mature. He supposed he shouldn't have been surprised. He'd met Katie and married her at age twenty-two and she'd been remarkably mature for her age.

"Nice to meet you, Heather. I'm Theo."

"So are you my mom's boyfriend?"

Theo coughed, heat from the very center of the Earth seeming to rush through him. He glanced over Heather's head to Katie, who wore a placid look, the fire in her eyes still dancing there.

"I guess so," he said, hoping that wouldn't add fuel to the flames. He and Katie hadn't exactly defined what they were. But boyfriend was better than ex-husband.

"Good," Heather said. "So I'll introduce you as that at the party. There's going to be a lot of girls there, and they'll want to know." She moved over to the kitchen area and opened a drawer before pulling out a notebook. "So I have a few questions for you." She perched on a barstool like she was Barbara Walters herself, about to conduct the most important interview of the century.

"Oh—questions." Theo looked at Katie, who wore a soft, fond smile on her face and watched her daughter. "All right. Let's do some questions." He moved into the kitchen too, and Katie offered water to everyone.

He declined, wondering if it was a mistake to do so, and sat at the bar with Heather. She launched into her first question with, "How old are you?"

"Forty-nine," he said.

"Any kids?"

"No."

She marked something in her notebook, and Theo relaxed, thinking this might be fun. "What do you do?"

"I build apps and websites," he said.

Heather looked up at him. "You do?"

"Yes, ma'am."

She threw a quick glance at her mom. "Amelia Grace's father does that."

"Oh." Theo sat up a little straighter. "What's her dad's name?"

"I don't know. Mom?"

"Collin Thresher," Katie said, almost as if she knew what kind of reaction she'd get from Theo.

He nearly tumbled off his barstool. "Collin Thresher?" he repeated. The surprise pouring through him couldn't have been any colder. He cleared his throat when he saw the curiosity on Heather's face.

"What?" she asked.

"Amelia Grace Thresher gets everything she wants," Katie said. "Remember that at the party. Both of you."

Theo knew exactly what she was saying, but he wasn't sure Heather did.

"Do you know him?" she asked.

"Well, kind of," Theo said. "He owns the second largest tech development firm in the state." Collin worked all over the islands, and Theo had heard he was after Island Airways too. Supreme satisfaction sang through him, but he quelled it. The paperwork wasn't signed yet, and until it was, nothing was official.

"They mostly work with banks and big companies," Theo said. "And as far as I know, Collin himself doesn't actually write the apps the way I do."

"What company do you own?" she asked.

Theo hesitated. "Well, I actually own more than one."

If Heather was surprised, she didn't show it. She waited, her pencil poised as if she'd write them all down and memorize them before the party started. Katie, however, had picked up a dish rag and she wiped in a circular motion over the same spot of countertop. Around and around, her eyes glued to Theo's.

"Okay," Heather said, clearly waiting for him to list them.

"So the biggest one is called Software Solutions," he said with a start. "And I own one called Singles Network. And one called The Web Developer." He cleared his throat and looked down at the counter. If someone had asked him last week which company brought in the most revenue, he'd have said Singles Network, as that branch of his business dealt with all the metropolitan areas served by the dating app.

But with Gladstone Financial and Island Airways on board, The Web Developer was definitely more lucrative this week.

"Do you have any pets?" Heather asked, and Katie sucked in a breath.

Theo caught her eye, but he couldn't interpret what she was trying to tell him, not the way he used to be able to. "No," he said slowly, something finally springing to his mind. "But I love cats."

Heather's whole face lit up and she said, "Really? Want to come meet my cats?" She set the notebook and pencil down and darted for the back door.

Theo was obviously meant to follow, and he looked at Katie, smiled, and said, "I guess I better go meet her cats."

"Thank you," Katie called after him, and Theo turned back to her from the doorway. "We'll talk later about your app, okay?"

She nodded, and he went into the backyard, which was clearly tended to and loved by Katie. He could see her careful hand in the way the bushes had been cut back. Feel her spirit in the bubbling water fountain.

"They don't come out much," Heather said. "But if you sit real quiet, you might be able to see one." She currently sat on the bottom step of the deck, and Theo went down and joined her.

"Where do they—ah. I see." He spotted the row of water bowls, and then the ones filled with food. "You do this? Every day?"

"I change the water in the morning," she said. "And the

food at night." She watched the yard, especially out by the trees.

"It sure is beautiful back here," he said, wondering if he should've gotten a house on the island. Someplace like this, where he could come out to the backyard and find peace and solace when he was working on a difficult puzzle or problem.

"My mom takes good care of the yard," Heather said. "She loves it."

"I can tell." And he knew that from the past too.

"She told me you guys were married."

Theo's eyebrows shot up. "She did?"

"Yeah." Heather sighed. "Said it was a long time ago."

"It was," he agreed. But his memories of her, of their marriage and time together, seemed to be so vivid. So real. So present.

"But you like her, right?" Heather asked.

"Yes, of course," Theo said, finding it easier to talk to Heather than he'd thought it would be.

"Okay, good," Heather said. "Because my dad is a real jerk."

Theo had not heard a single thing about her father, and he didn't want to hear it from her anyway. "I—I'm sorry to hear that."

"Look!" She pointed, her voice dropping as she whispered, "There's one there. That one's called Boots, because he has white fur on his paws."

Theo couldn't see a darn thing, but he nodded like he could. "Oh, I see him." He hoped he could make this birthday party fun for Heather. She was a sweet girl, and he liked her already.

"Time for the party," Katie called, and Heather turned toward her.

"Mom, you scared off Boots." She huffed and got up. Stomping up the steps, she said, "And we barely got to see him."

"Sorry," Katie said in a tone that indicated she couldn't care less about the stray cat in her trees. Theo chuckled as he came back to the deck too.

"This place is amazing," he said. "When do you have time to do this?" He paused in front of her, finding her absolutely breathtaking in this sunlight.

She gazed up at him, those oceanic eyes pulling him in, in, in like she was a strong tide. "We spend time on things we care about."

Theo wondered if she was lecturing him or not. "Wise words," he said. "Do you think I'll survive this?" He leaned closer, inhaling the sweet scent of Katie's hair.

"Oh, I'm sure you'll be fine." She grinned at him and brushed her fingers against his. "I can't wait to hear all about it."

Theo had his doubts, but he buried them deep, something he'd gotten very good at doing over the years. When a deal fell through, he only allowed himself to wallow in doubt and disappointment for a short time. Sometimes a day. Once he was down and out for a few months—and as he dug in his pocket for his keys he realized that was when Katie had left him and his second business had failed, all within a month of each other.

"Is that your car?" Heather stood at the top of the front steps, staring at his convertible.

"Yes," he said. "I can put the top up so your hair doesn't get all messed up."

She looked at him with awe in her expression. "Amelia Grace is going to freak when she sees that." She skipped down the steps, a bump of pure glee in her movement.

"Why?" he asked, following her.

"She's always bragging about how awesome her dad's cars are," she said.

Theo got in and started the car. "Seatbelts," he said. He backed out of Katie's driveway, catching sight of her standing in the doorway, her arms clenched around her middle and a worried look on her face. He wanted to reassure her that they'd be fine, but he just focused on the road.

"So," he said. "It seems like you don't even like Amelia Grace all that much." He watched her out of his peripheral vision, hoping he wasn't overstepping his bounds.

"She's all right," Heather said.

"Then why do you want to go to this party so bad?" he asked.

"I don't know," Heather said. "It's just...she's friends with everyone, and if you're not friends with her, there's not anyone else to be friends with."

"What about boys?" Theo asked.

"My mom says I'm not allowed to date until I'm twenty-five."

Theo tipped his head back and laughed, though that

sounded exactly like something Katie would say. "You can be friends with a boy without dating him."

"Yeah, I know." But Heather didn't say anything else, and Theo followed the GPS to get to the Thresher's house. As he pulled behind the other cars, a trickle of unrest ran through him. But he straightened his shoulders and handed Heather the birthday present she'd brought with her.

"All right," he said. "Let's do this."

NINE

KATIE DIDN'T KNOW what to do with herself. Saturday evening without Heather. Without any chores. Without any obligations. She thought about calling Claire but dismissed the idea quickly. She just wanted to change into a pair of pants that had a stretchy waistband, dig around in the freezer for some ice cream, and find something romantic to watch on TV.

So she did all of that, enjoying every moment of the peace and solitude. Every once in a while, a nervous thought about Heather entered her mind, but she pushed them away. Both Theo and her daughter had phones, and if something was wrong, Katie was sure one of them would let her know.

But it was a birthday party. What could possibly go wrong?

Katie knew, though. Amelia Grace could be wonderful

and kind, pay all kinds of attention to Heather like they were best friends, and then the next day at school, she'd act like she didn't even know Heather existed.

Katie suspected there were some problems behind the perfect front doors at the Thresher mansion, and she'd tried to tell Heather that some girls were just insecure. But Heather didn't want to hear anything bad about Amelia Grace.

So Katie had stopped talking about it, choosing instead to follow Heather's lead, answer her questions, and listen to her if she brought up the other girl.

It seemed like hours and hours had passed before the front door opened, and Heather yelled, "Mom!" Her footsteps ran toward her, and Katie had just gotten herself to the edge of the bed when her daughter appeared in the doorway.

No tears.

Relief cascaded through Katie, and she asked, "How was it?"

Heather looked like someone had stuffed the sun down her throat. She glowed in a way Katie had never seen before. Ever.

"It was so great, Mom. Theo is good at everything. He won like, five games, and he drove the nicest car there, and everyone wanted to go for a ride in it, and it made Amelia Grace *sooo* mad." She laughed and rushed into the room. She jumped onto the bed beside Katie and started up again.

"And then her dad said something about work, and

Theo said at least he could afford to pay his bills. Her dad turned so red. It was awesome." She lay back on the bed, a sigh hissing from her mouth.

"So you made Amelia Grace mad at her party," Katie said, trying to piece everything together. "I thought you wanted to be friends with her."

"She was so rude to Francine. You should've seen her. She took a cracker and crushed it up in her fist and then dumped it in Francine's hair. And laughed about it."

"Oh, wow," Katie said, knowing that every story had a dozen sides. "Why would she do that?"

"Because Francine said she likes *Moana* more than *Frozen*." Heather made a scoffing noise. "She's just mean, Mom."

"Again, I thought you *wanted* to be friends with her." Katie twisted, trying to get a good view of her daughter's face.

"I guess. I don't know. Theo says I shouldn't have to be friends with her just because she's popular. That a lot of the other girls probably feel like I do about her."

"Oh, Theo said that, huh?" Heather looked happy, truly happy, like she really had enjoyed herself at the party, despite the crackers and Amelia Grace acting like a spoiled brat.

"So anyway, I helped Francine get all the crackers out of her hair, and we went out front for a minute. That's when more girls came, and Theo offered rides. It was fine."

"Knock, knock," Theo said, and Katie whipped her attention back to the doorway. He stood there, tall and silver and gorgeous, and Katie wanted nothing more than to kiss him. Tip up on her toes and whisper, "Thank you," and then *kiss him.*

Maybe winning all the games and stealing the show with his fancy convertible wasn't the smartest move. But giving Heather the confidence to be her own person was worth something. Katie would like nothing more than for her to break away from Amelia Grace and start to be happy with herself just the way she was.

But she knew better than most how hard change was, that moving away from something familiar and comfortable would make a person quite *un*comfortable. And very few people chose to be uncomfortable when they could have something easier.

"Hey." She stood and ran her hands through her hair. "How was the party?"

"So good." He held up a paper bag. "I won like ten candy bars."

"They let you have them?"

"All the other dads were playing."

"You should see him play lawn darts, Mom. He's so good." Heather bounced to the edge of the bed and said, "I'm going to go feed the cats. Then can I make dinner?"

"Yeah, sure," Katie said.

Heather strode over to Theo and turned back to Katie. "Can Theo stay for dinner?"

"Uh." The word fell from Katie's lips, and she looked to Theo. "I'm sure Theo is busy tonight."

"I'm not busy," he said, a big grin appearing on his face.

"Can he stay, Mom?" Heather asked, which only annoyed Katie. She didn't like being put on the spot. If she said no, she'd be the bad guy.

And she didn't want to say no anyway. She just didn't want to seem overeager and blurt out, "Yes, of course."

So she said, "I guess," and left it at that.

"Thanks, Mom." Heather ran back over to her and wrapped her in a hug. "Thanks for getting someone to go with me." She smiled up at her, and it was those moments that made all the work it took to be a mother worthwhile.

"Did you tell Theo thank you?"

She skipped over to Theo and wrapped her arms around him too. Heather sucked in a breath and held it, her eyes widening at the sight of her daughter hugging a man. The last time she'd done that, it was to her father on the night he was arrested.

Flashbacks ran through Katie's mind, images flashing one after the other. What a terrible night that had been.

And this evening was the complete opposite of that.

"Thank you for taking me, Theo."

"Anytime, sweets. I had fun." Theo beamed at her, seemingly at ease with the hugging, even going with a term of endearment. Katie shook her head. How long had this party been? Had she lost days or weeks of her life? Maybe she'd simply consumed too much chocolate brownie ice cream.

Heather left the room, and Katie waited until she heard the backdoor close before even breathing again.

She realized Theo stood on the threshold of her bedroom, and he wasn't coming any closer. She jerked into a walk and crossed the room to him. "Let's hear your version of the party."

"It was fun," he said again, stepping into the hall. He went into the living room and sat near the middle of the couch, leaving her very few choices for where to sit. Feeling bold and bit out of control—again, probably from all the sugar in that ice cream—she sank onto the sofa right next to him.

He lifted his arm and curled it around her shoulders like he'd been doing so for the past two decades. "I don't think any of the girls there actually like Amelia Grace," he said. "But they all act like they do."

"Mm." Katie basked in the warmth from his body. "Did you really give rides to fifth graders in your convertible?"

He chuckled, the sound low and deep and wonderful. "Probably a bad idea, huh?"

Katie giggled with him, snuggling a little deeper into his side. "I don't know. Probably worth it."

Something banged outside, and she lifted her head as if she could see out the window from the couch, but she couldn't.

"What is she going to make for dinner?" he asked. "She told me she likes to cook, but are we talking like peanut butter sandwiches or like a real meal?"

"She'll probably do something like hamburgers or hot dogs tonight," Katie said. "But she does cook a lot. Pancakes, pork chops, spaghetti. Stuff like that."

"That's impressive."

"She likes it."

With his free hand, he reached over and took one her hands. "So…what's the deal with her dad?"

Katie spasmed. "What do you mean?"

"She didn't say a whole lot," he said, his words rushing a bit. "But she said he was a real jerk, and when someone asked her about her real dad, she said she doesn't see him anymore."

Katie inhaled slowly, infusing reason into her thoughts. "His name was—is—Ray. Ray Harrison. We were married for five years." She gave a mirthless laugh. "I can't seem to stay married for longer than five years." She hadn't realized that coincidence until that moment, and it stung her over and over again.

Theo said nothing, just rubbed his thumb over her fingers again and again.

"He's in prison," Katie said, going straight to the point. "He was stealing and distributing and addicted to prescription painkillers. Had a whole apothecary in a storage unit. Biggest drug bust of its kind in Kansas in a decade." Her voice had slipped into robotic mode, and she hated the sound of it.

"I filed for divorce, took Heather, and left the state. Left the mainland, actually. We've been here ever since."

"Katie," he said softly, tenderly. "I'm so sorry."

"Things happen," she said as if the loss of her marriage didn't matter to her. But it had mattered, and she'd been devastated for a long time. Sometimes, she still had flashes of what her life could be like if Ray had just been a man who worked nine to five, came home for dinner, and went to watch Heather's soccer games on the weekends.

Of course, here in Hawaii, she'd taken up cooking and painting, leaving the group sports in Kansas.

"No," Theo said, his mouth dipping dangerously close to her ear. "Not those kinds of things, Katie."

"Maybe not."

"Does she ever talk to him?"

"He sends cards from time to time," Katie said. "She seems to be doing okay, most of the time. We both are."

"She's a great kid."

"Thank you."

The back door opened, and Katie sprang out of Theo's embrace as if the person entering were her mother. "All fed?" she asked.

"Yes, but I dropped that stupid lid again, and I can't get it out of the bushes. They're too prickly." She held up her hand, which had blood on it. "I need a band aid."

"I got it," Katie said, heading for the bathroom. "Be right back." She collected the band aid but stood in front of the mirror. She looked like she could use a nap—or that she'd been lying in bed, which of course, she had been.

She hadn't told anyone about Ray in so long, and it felt like the oxygen had been simultaneously sucked out of the air but also infused into her lungs. Sharing the burden she carried made it lighter, and she trusted Theo explicitly.

A small smile touched her mouth, and she reached up and traced her fingers along her bottom lip. Could she kiss Theo tonight before he left?

The thought rooted itself in her mind and wouldn't let go, and all she wanted to do was kiss Theo and let him know how much she liked him.

Maybe, she told the voice in her head that wouldn't let go of the idea. *Maybe.*

TEN

THEO BASKED in the family atmosphere at Katie's house. Everything about her place felt different from his, and it wasn't just the physical surroundings. His life was sterile, made up of numbers and accounts, parentheses and colons, code and running and phone calls.

But this house was full of life, the smell of hamburgers grilling in the backyard and music playing from a Bluetooth speaker on top of the fridge and the island breeze coming in the open windows.

He sure had enjoyed himself at the party, and not only because it had been quite the treat to upstage Collin Thresher, even for a moment. But he liked talking to Heather and seeing her come alive.

Katie took forever getting a band aid, and by the time she returned, Heather had the bleeding under control with a paper towel wrapped around her finger. With the bandage in place, she opened a drawer and took out a knife. Katie seemed unalarmed by this, but Theo marveled as she cut vegetables for a salad. She ran in and out of the house, once with an oversized spatula, then with a plate with cheese slices on it, then to get the burgers when they were finished.

His to-do list contained at least a dozen items, and he didn't care about any of them, not right now. He'd had no idea his life had such a giant hole in it—until now. He hadn't known what shape it was or what could fill it.

But he knew now.

A family.

His heart beat irregularly, increasing when Heather said, "Okay, dinner's ready."

Katie, who had taken a spot on the loveseat opposite him and closed her eyes, opened them and blinked. She stood without looking at Theo and asked, "Should I make punch?"

"Sure," Heather said, reaching into the fridge and pulling out ketchup, mustard, and mayo.

Theo joined them in the kitchen, but he stayed on the side of the bar where there was no activity. "This is amazing," he said, truly feeling the wonder of watching a ten-year-old cook while her mother dozed on the couch.

"Do you cook, Theo?" Heather asked, almost a different person from the Barbara Walters wannabe from earlier. Her eyes held more life, and she looked so much happier, so much more carefree.

"A little," he said, not wanting to admit that the most action his kitchen saw was him making coffee in the morning. And the evening, if he was being honest. Sometimes the day didn't have enough hours, and he had more work than time.

Katie snorted and pulled a large spoon from a drawer. As she stirred the punch, she said, "He does not cook. Not even a little."

"Hey," he said, glancing at Heather. For some reason, he wanted this child to like him. "I may have taken a lesson or two in the last twenty years. You don't know."

"Have you?" Katie grinned at him.

"No," he said with a smile, a chuckle not far behind. "But I could have."

Katie laughed too, put the spoon in the sink, and picked up a plate. "What kind of cheese is this?"

"Muenster," Heather said. "It's all we had."

Katie flashed her daughter a quick smile. "It's great."

"Oh, Mom, I almost forgot." Heather started with her bun, putting condiments on it. "Francine asked if I could sleep over sometime."

"Tonight?"

"I don't think so," Heather said, shooting a glance at Theo. But he hadn't stayed glued to her side, and he had no idea what Francine had said.

He too picked up a plate and a hamburger bun and started preparing it, simply listening to the two of them talk about Francine, her family, and if a sleepover was a good idea.

"Please, Mom," Heather said, and Theo heard all the pleading undertones. She sat at the table and looked at her mom with puppy dog eyes. "You can call her mom and talk to her. She said she has this cool outdoor tree house to sleep in."

"I'll think about it," Katie said. Theo finished with his sandwich and joined them at the table.

One bite into the burger, and he moaned. "This is great," he said, not caring that his mouth was full of food. Everything about this situation was foreign to him. He usually ate at his desk, perhaps with Ben munching on something across from him as they talked about a client or worked through a piece of code that was giving them fits.

But a real conversation, with real, home-cooked food? It felt like he'd blasted off to another planet.

The conversation moved on, and he was happy to listen to Katie and Heather talk about school and home-work and their schedule for the next week. He heard them make plans to go out to Lightning Point the following day, and he almost asked if he could join them.

He'd never been out to the tip of the island where light-ning seemed called to strike, and he'd always wanted to go. Not during a storm, of course, but to see the area, talk to the glassmaker who'd started putting rods in the sand so she could then collect the results.

From what he'd heard around the island in the short time he'd been here was that it was pretty rare that anything ever came of the lightning strikes. Despite the artists efforts to get a piece of petrified lightning, the rumors were she never had.

Still, it was a cool place, with dozens of documented lightning strikes over the years.

Theo said nothing. If they wanted him to come, they'd

invite him. And neither one of them did, so he finished his hamburger and got up to get more potato chips.

"Where did you live before you moved here?" Heather asked him.

"Texas," he said. "And you guys?"

"Kansas," she said, shooting a look at Katie.

"Did you like Kansas?" he asked, sensing he was on thin ice with this topic.

"I don't know," Heather said. "I was really little when we left."

He looked at Katie, and she startled. "Oh, yeah. Um, yes. I liked Kansas. It's...different than here."

"What took you to Kansas?" he asked her. They'd met at Texas A&M, fell in love, gotten married, and moved to the Dallas-Fort Worth area after that. Her parents lived in Texas, and he couldn't imagine her ever leaving the state.

But obviously, there was a lot he couldn't imagine that had actually happened.

"Work," she said. "After I...." Worry darted through her eyes, and Theo wished he could erase it. Tell her that she could talk about their past relationship, that he was okay.

"After we got divorced, you...." he prompted.

She smiled, but it was short-lived. "I went back to school, actually. I got a nursing certificate, and then a job in Topeka. That's what took me to Kansas."

He dusted his hands of potato chip crumbs. "And yet you now own and operate a cleaning business."

"Nursing is great," she said. "Don't get me wrong. But it was...exhausting. I needed a break."

"Everything changed when we moved here," Heather said.

"Heather," Katie said sharply, drawing the girl's attention to her. "Why don't you go finish your art project and then get in the tub? I'll clean up tonight."

"Really?" Heather grinned and bolted from the table like it had caught fire. "Thanks, Mom." She left, and Theo watched Katie as relief and relaxation spread through her again.

"You can tell me about Kansas," he said softly, reaching for her hand.

She let him take it, and gladness poured through him. He liked her so much—always had. And it was a very slippery slope from there to falling in love with her all over again.

"After Ray got arrested and I found out what he'd really been doing to make money, I decided to abandon everything in my life." She glanced at him, those big eyes calling to him again. "Except Heather, of course."

"Of course," he murmured.

"So I closed that chapter. Sold the house and pretty much most of what we owned. No car, no knickknacks, nothing. Well, I kept one photo album."

Theo very much wanted to see what was in it. If he could condense his whole life into one album, what would it have in it?

"And we left. Left the state. Left our friends. Left the Mainland. Left the job. And we came here, and we opened a new chapter. Started over." She squeezed his hand, and he met her eyes again. "So yeah. Everything changed when we moved here. And Heather was only five, but she's not stupid, and we've talked a lot about Ray and why I decided to bring us here to start over."

Theo didn't know what to say. He smiled at her and kept a tight grip on her fingers. "It must've been hard," was all he could come up with.

"Hardest thing I've ever done." She nodded, focusing on the tabletop.

"Harder than leaving me?" he asked, unsure of why he'd asked.

"Oh, Theo." She looked at him, raw emotion on her face. "That was really hard too." Her voice broke on the last word. "But we didn't have kids, and my parents were willing to help."

"They wouldn't help when your husband was arrested?"

"They never liked Ray," Katie said. "And Daddy was sick, and my mother...well, she didn't have it in her at the time. That was another reason I came here. I didn't want to add to her burden."

"I didn't know your dad was sick. Is he okay now?"

"Seems to be."

"You don't know?"

"He and Mama got divorced a few years ago. He moved to Florida, and I don't hear from him much."

"Wow." Theo didn't know what to do with that news. "They had to be married what? Forty years?"

"Almost fifty," she said. "Mama moved to Ohio and lives near Janelle."

"Do you talk to your sister much?"

"A little." Katie sounded sad, and Theo didn't like it. He stood and started clearing the plates. He may not cook and clean for himself, but that didn't mean he didn't know how. He'd spent plenty of years eating cold cereal for every meal, hoping his new idea would bring home more than a few hundred bucks.

They cleaned up the kitchen together, and he felt his time with her ending. What a perfect day it had been, and Theo closed his eyes and took a long breath of air.

"Want to sit on the deck for a few minutes?" Katie asked.

"Absolutely." He took her hand and they went outside together. A swing sat on the edge of the deck, and Katie headed that way.

Once they were settled, she pushed gently with her foot, setting them in motion. The sun had started to set, and the last rays of its light painted the sky with blue and purple, red and gold, orange and white.

He sighed, more peace filling him now than ever before. Katie laid her head against his shoulder, and he squeezed her hand. He wasn't sure why, but he felt the need to ask, "I really am your boyfriend, aren't I?"

She lifted her head and looked at him. Nothing was said, but Theo could read her expression—he always could—and she was definitely saying yes.

He bent down, hesitated for another moment, and then let his eyes drift closed as he touched his mouth to hers. Instant fire exploded through every cell of his body, making his blood run faster and his pulse accelerate.

He brought one hand to her face, holding her there,

breathing with her as the kiss deepened and lengthened. He'd kissed her so many times in the past, but this felt like opening a new chapter in his life, like every other kiss was only preparation for this one.

"Can I see you tomorrow?" he asked, breathless and desperate for more time with her. Even if he got twenty-four hours a day with her again, it wouldn't be enough.

She kissed him again, both of her hands moving through his hair, her fingernails along his scalp sending shockwaves down his back. She tipped her head back, and Theo moved his mouth to her neck.

"We're going to Lightning Point tomorrow," she whispered.

"Mm." He claimed her mouth again, very aware that he was making out with her on her back deck, with her daughter just inside the house. And it felt good. It felt right. She was the missing piece in his life, and he absolutely had to have her back.

He finally pulled away and tucked her into his side. It took several minutes for his heart rate to quiet and his thoughts to align. "So it's a public place," he said. "If I happened to show up say, around noon...."

"Maybe one," Katie said, pushing them softly every time they swung forward.

The silence between them was beautiful, and as dusk settled, Theo asked, "This isn't crazy, is it?"

"What?"

"Us," he said. "Do people get second chances twenty years later?"

Something banged inside the house, and Katie looked

that way. She stalled the motion of the swing and stood up, pulling him up after her. She wrapped her arms around him and gazed up at him. "They sure seem to, don't they?" A smile touched her mouth just before she tipped up on her toes and kissed him again.

This time, it wasn't as passionate, wasn't as powerful, but it was simple and sweet and that was almost as wonderful. "I don't think this is crazy," she murmured, stepping back. "Lightning Point. One o'clock." Then she turned and went inside, only looking back to wave one final time.

Theo exhaled, his emotions and his thoughts running rampant. He didn't normally spend Sundays exploring the island or relaxing. But it didn't matter. Anything and everything could be shifted so he could be at Lightning Point by one o'clock tomorrow.

At least he hoped so.

ELEVEN

HOURS AFTER HEATHER had been tucked in, Katie lay awake in her own bed. She relived that kiss in the swing over and over, her body too warm. So then she'd fling off her covers, get cold, and pull them all back on again.

So the relationship with Theo was a bit crazy, she supposed. All she knew was that she didn't want it to end. That thought scared her enough to make her shiver, and then a whole new cycle of questions, doubts, and reassurances circled through her mind.

Sunday was the only day she really got any rest. She and Heather almost always went somewhere, spent time together, just the two of them. Had she ruined that by unofficially inviting Theo? Should she text him and cancel?

She finally fell asleep with those thoughts in her head, and when Heather woke her in the morning, she groaned and rolled over.

"What time is it?"

"Almost nine, Mom." She leaned onto the bed. "I was thinking."

"Oh, boy." Katie smiled as Heather lay down in bed beside her. "What were you thinking about?"

"We should've invited Theo to Lightning Point," Heather said. "We sat there and talked about it right in front of him, and Amelia Grace has done that to me before, and it hurts my feelings."

Her daughter snuggled deeper into her side, and Katie marveled at how she'd gotten such a sweet girl. "I can text him," she said, stroking Heather's hair. "Want me to braid your hair today?"

"Yeah, can you do two French braids into a ponytail?"

"Sure." Katie loved the laziness of Sunday mornings, lying in bed with the sunlight splashing through the windows. "You like Theo, then?"

"Yeah, Mom. He's great."

He's great.

Katie thought so too, and a measure of joy she hadn't felt in her life in so, so long filled her heart. "And you're okay that we're dating?"

"You've gone out with other guys, Mom."

"One or two," Katie said. "And this is…different." She didn't need to discuss every aspect of her relationship with Theo with her ten-year-old. "This is more serious. We're together, and I won't be going out with other guys. Just him. You know what that means?"

Heather pushed herself up on one elbow and looked at Heather. "Are you going to marry him again?"

Katie scoffed like the very idea was ridiculous. But what did she think would happen? Only two avenues existed for a relationship like the one she was cultivating with Theo—a painful break-up or a marriage.

She sobered. "I don't know, sweetheart. We're just starting out. Getting to know each other again. That type of thing."

Heather shrugged and scooted to the edge of the bed. "I like him, and I get what dating means." She headed for the door. "I'm going to pack some sandwiches. You have to get all the gear."

Katie groaned, but it was more in jest than actually not wanting to get together all their beach stuff. She stayed in bed for a few more minutes, then she got up and raked her fingers through her hair. After twisting it into a messy bun on top of her head, she dug around in her drawers for a swimming suit she could potentially wear in front of Theo.

Impossible.

There was no way she could wear any of them in front of him. They all screamed *mom here! Middle-aged mom!*

Which of course, she was. And when she went to the beach, she normally wasn't there to catch the eye of any eligible bachelors. She wouldn't be today either, unless Theo counted.

And wow, thinking about the kisses they'd shared the previous evening, he counted. He counted a whole lot.

She slammed her drawer closed and turned around, her thoughts barreling down a track she wasn't sure had a happy ending. So she wouldn't wear a swimming suit today, that was all. Big deal.

She found a pair of jean shorts that were a half a size too small and pulled them on. She stood in front of the full-length mirror in her bathroom for far too long, trying to decide if she looked good or if she was trying too hard.

In the end, she went with the denim and paired the shorts with a tank top that would've allowed her to blend into the Hawaiian nights. Halfway between navy and black, she liked the way the top gave her curves more oomph and somehow made her look less like she needed to trim off ten pounds. Okay, fine, maybe twenty pounds.

When she finally went into the kitchen to make coffee, Heather sat on the couch, her backpack packed and zipped closed beside her. The rolling cooler waited beside the island, clearly ready too.

"Ready already?" she asked, reaching for the coffee grounds.

"Yes, Mom."

"It's barely ten," Katie said. "I just texted Theo and he said he can't meet us until one." So she'd told a fib. It wouldn't end the world.

"And you have more makeup on than I've ever seen."

"I do not." Katie turned her back on her daughter and busied herself with filling the coffee pot with water. Maybe she should take the makeup down a notch. Most of it would be hidden behind her sunglasses anyway.

She shook off the self-conscious thoughts, telling herself that her ten-year-old didn't get to make her feel like her adult choices were wrong.

"Besides, it'll be cold if we go too early." So she puttered around the kitchen, putting together a breakfast of a slice of toast and a cup of peaches. When her coffee was ready, she loaded it with cream and sugar and sat at the table by herself.

Katie tried really hard not to work on Sundays, as she really needed one day away from Clean Sweep completely. That was one reason she and Heather usually planned their outings for Sundays.

"All right," she said about half an hour later. "I'll go get the stuff packed up. We'll be ready to go soon."

Heather grunted, and Katie left her in the house to go see what she'd done with the beach chairs and towels and bag. Of course she knew where it all was. The chairs hung on the pegs she'd had her neighbor come install for her. The beach bag waited below them, right where she'd left it last time they'd used it.

And it had everything in it she needed: sunscreen, sunglasses, umbrella stand, a portable shovel, her beach hat, and her water bottle. She collected hers and Heather's and sat them on the steps leading back into the house. She replaced the wet wipes with new ones and shook out the sand from last weekend.

When everything was ready, she tossed it all in the back of her car and went back inside to fill up the water bottles. "All right," she said. "Let's go." As she led Heather outside, she had the idea that she should text Theo and tell him they were leaving now. "Let me just let Theo know we'll be there earlier."

She started the car and adjusted the air before pulling out her phone and sending him the message. She didn't even have time to breathe before his return message said, *Great I'll see you when you get here.*

She stared at her phone. *Are you there already?*

Maybe.

She imagined his face wearing a coy smile and a hint of mischief in those ice blue eyes. She giggled and shook her head. It wasn't until Heather said, "What?" that Katie remembered she wasn't alone in the car.

She almost dropped her phone in her haste to hide it from her daughter. "Nothing." She pressed the power button to make it go to sleep, then she set it in the cup holder. "Let's go. Theo said he'd meet us there."

Driving around Getaway Bay was one of the things Katie loved best about her life in the islands. Everything smelled fresh every morning. The trees stayed green year-round. And the breeze coming off the ocean reminded her that it was okay to have an easy day once a week.

She kept the windows rolled down and went five below the speed limit as she rounded the island and continued on toward Lightning Point.

Her mind also stayed on a slower track, something for which Katie was grateful. She'd had a busy day yesterday and told Theo a lot of things. He'd reacted the way she'd expected him to—calm, in control, no judgment.

She hadn't been afraid to tell him, exactly. Maybe just embarrassed. But he'd been nothing but kind, and she hoped to get a few answers of her own today.

When she finally pulled into the parking lot, the clock had ticked closer to eleven-thirty, and she found only a few cars. "Not very popular today," she said.

"Nope."

She pulled beside the sportiest car in the lot, a model with only letters and numbers instead of a name. "This one has to be Theo's," she said. She hadn't known he was a big car buff. When they'd been married, he talked constantly about achieving his dreams of becoming a billionaire by age twenty-seven. Then twenty-eight. He was good at a lot of things, but building a business that actually made money wasn't one of them—at least that was how it had seemed.

He'd talked about the life he wanted to have with her, the land in Texas, even a fancy yacht so he could cruise around the Gulf of Mexico. But cars?

She got out and looked at the sleek, black sports car. Definitely Theo's. "Come on, Heather," she called, moving around to the trunk of her ordinary car. She wondered if vehicles felt jealousy when they were parked next to much nicer, newer, fancier models.

Probably not.

Katie collected all of their gear, and Heather shouldered her backpack and pulled the cooler behind her. They'd only taken a few steps when Theo came jogging toward them. He wore a pair of board shorts that had every color in the rainbow in them, as well as a gray tank top with wide straps and the word CODE on it.

"There you are," he said, smiling. He was tan, and tall, and so tantalizing that Katie wanted to step into him, inhaled the saltiness of his skin and then kiss him. She remembered she was with her daughter at the last moment. "Let me take something."

She passed him the beach bag and the umbrella, keeping the chairs and her purse. "Thanks. You look good."

"You too." He stood there staring at her, that silly smile on his face.

"Where's your stuff?" Heather asked, moving past them and looking out onto the beach. She shivered. "It's cold here."

"I told you we didn't need to come so early," Katie said. "It'll warm up as the sun rises higher."

"It's not bad, actually," Theo said. "The breeze dies and then it gets hot." He started toward a single beach towel in the sand. "I'm out there. There are a couple of sand castle artists here. I've been watching them."

When they arrived at his tiny patch of sand, she found a single canister of sunscreen nearby, as well as his phone and a portable charger. At least she knew his priorities now.

"The umbrella is nice if it's not too windy," she said. "I have a portable shovel."

"Sounds about right." Theo grinned at her and got to work. In a matter of minutes, they had their spot staked out, and Katie relaxed in her chair with a sigh.

"You've always loved the beach," he said.

"True."

"Mom, I'm going to go out, okay?" Heather pulled her T-shirt over her head and tossed it on the blanket.

She started for the water before waiting for Katie to say, "Okay, watch out for the tide!"

Theo reached for her hand before Heather's gangly legs had taken her even two steps. "Hey, how'd you sleep?"

"Honestly?"

"I think we're way past the point of being dishonest with each other." He looked at her, but she couldn't see those glorious eyes behind his shades.

"I suppose." She focused on the waves undulating in the distance. "Not great, actually. A certain, handsome man kept me awake past my bedtime. Seems he forgot I need my beauty sleep now that I'm getting older."

Theo burst out laughing, and Katie couldn't help joining him. He pulled on her hand, a clear invitation for her to join him on the blanket. She resisted for about four seconds, then she slid next to him, curling easily into his side like she'd done many times before.

"I missed you," he whispered.

"It's been a few hours."

"Still." His lips found hers easily, and he kissed her slowly, almost like he'd forgotten what it was like and needed to explore her mouth all over again. She melted into him easily, the way she always had and tried to hold onto every single second.

"Mm, I think you missed me too."

"Maybe," she said, and he chuckled, the sound deep and delicious as it traveled through his chest and into hers. "I have a question for you."

"Oh, boy."

"It's not bad." Well, maybe it was. She didn't know. "Why didn't you ever get married again? I mean, it's been twenty years, and you're good looking...." She let her words die there, half hoping he'd say he'd simply never gotten over her.

"I don't know," he said. "Never met the right woman."

"Would you?"

"Would I what? Meet the right woman?"

"Get married again," she said

"Depends," he said, kneading her closer and keeping his fingers on her upper arm tight. "On who's wearing the white dress at the end of the aisle."

Katie didn't ask him her next question—*what if it was me?*—because she already knew the answer. He'd married her once, and he'd likely do so again—if it came to that.

But that's a long way from now, Katie told herself. After all, she wasn't twenty-two this time, and she had Heather to consider in every single thing she did.

TWELVE

THEO ENJOYED HOLDING KATIE, and he liked even more that she didn't jump out of his embrace when her daughter came back dripping wet. "Mom, I'm starving."

"Then eat something."

Heather opened the cooler they'd brought and started digging around.

"What did you make?" he asked her. He hadn't thought past a towel, his sunglasses, and the sunscreen he'd found at a convenience store on the way over.

"Ham and cheese," Heather said, holding up a sandwich. "And tuna with lettuce and tomato." She pulled out another sandwich and kept that one, putting the ham and cheese back. Theo smiled at her as she took the beach chair in the sun.

"See? It's not too bad, is it?" he asked.

"The water is choppy," she said.

"I heard they're doing a demo on petrified lightning later," Theo said. He hadn't heard, but he'd already been to the visitor's center and the worker there had told him.

"Seen it," Heather said in a bored voice. Theo shut up after that, trying to figure out how to get her to open up to him like she had the day before. In his arms, Katie lay very still.

"Is she mad at me?" Theo asked.

Katie's shoulders started to shake, and while she tried to muffle her giggles, he could clearly hear them.

"What?" he asked.

"Nothing."

But it was clearly something. "Come on," he said, keeping his voice low and one eye on Heather. He wasn't an expert on the opposite sex by any stretch of the imagination, but he knew he'd never get Katie to be his if her daughter wasn't on board.

"She's not mad at you," Katie said, her breath tickling his collarbone. "She's ten."

He blinked, trying to understand.

"Sometimes she feels like talking, and sometimes she doesn't," Katie continued. "It only gets worse, I've heard." She laughed again, the sound of it light as soft rain.

Theo wanted to kiss her again, but he refrained. Instead, he said, "Well, this is my first time here, so I'm going to go to the demo."

"This is your first time here?" Heather asked.

Theo looked back at her. "Yeah. You wanna show me around?"

"Yeah, I do." She shoved her sandwich back in the bag and got to her feet. "Are you wearing a swimming suit?"

"Yes, ma'am." No need to tell anyone that he'd bought it that morning, five minutes after the department store had opened. At least he'd remembered to bring a pair of scissors so he could remove the tag.

He gently removed himself from Katie's embrace and stood up. "I guess I'm getting the tour."

"Have fun," Katie said, clearly not going to join them. She reached into her bag and pulled out a paperback book. Theo gaped at her, wanting to educate her on the beauty of an e-reader and how many books she could fit onto it.

"Let's go." Heather danced through the sand in front of him. "Okay, so there's this swimming spot that's great. It's just down the beach a bit."

Theo laughed and followed her, wondering if he should've brought a towel with him. But Heather didn't have one, so he figured he was okay. He let her lead him around the point, listening to her talk about the fish she'd seen here before, and why she liked this swimming spot more than others.

They laughed and played in the water, and he asked her, "Does your mom ever come out and swim?"

"Usually, yeah." She shaded her eyes and looked toward shore, though Katie had to be a dot on the horizon to his right from this spot. "She didn't even put on her suit today, though."

Theo had noticed a very short pair of denim shorts that looked like she'd poured herself into them. And he'd liked them. He kept everything to himself though, and said, "Hm. Why's that, do you think?"

"Because she wants to look good for you," Heather said simply.

Theo needed to change the subject, and fast. "Is there a good place for snorkeling here?" he asked.

"No, the water's too rough," she said. "The best snorkeling is on the beach between the two bays."

"Will you take me sometime?" he asked.

"Yeah, sure," she said, a happy smile on her face. "I don't have gear though."

"Me either. I can get us some."

When Theo's shoulders felt like they were frying, he made Heather get out of the water and they trudged back through the sand to where Katie lay asleep.

He wrapped himself in a towel and checked his phone. He'd missed four calls from Ben, and the petrified lightning demo was about to begin. "You sure you don't want to go to the demo?" he asked at the same time his stomach growled.

"It's not that great," Heather said. "Honest, it's not. You can look the same stuff up online."

He glanced toward the visitor's center, thinking, thinking. "I need to make a call," he said. "I'll walk over there and see what's going on."

"Okay." Heather was back in her chair, this time with a can of soda in her hand.

"You should put on more sunscreen," he said, picking up his can. He needed to as well, and as soon as he was dry enough to do it, he would.

"Okay," she said, but she didn't make a move to actually put any more on.

He walked away, already dialing Ben. "Hey," he said when he picked up. "What's going on?'

"Where are you?"

"I went out to Lightning Point. What's going on?" he asked again.

"Lawrence was looking for you."

Alarm pulled through Theo. "Why? Everything with his project is on track. We're not even supposed to meet for another month."

"I don't know. He came by the office and said you weren't answering at your place. So I got the key and came up and you were gone."

"I leave my condo sometimes." Theo wanted to laugh, but at the same time, he knew he didn't get out much.

"Obviously. Are you with Katie?"

"Yes." He turned back to where she still slept in the sand. "And you freaked me out. You realize you called *four* times? I thought Island Airways was backing out."

Ben laughed, which only annoyed Theo further. "I'm hanging up now," he said. "*Text* me if you need me." He hung up before Ben finished chuckling, and he went to see if the petrified lightning demo was as bad as Heather claimed.

———

Tuesday came, and the Island Airways paperwork got signed. He and Ben scheduled a group call with all the team lead developers in Dallas, and they had a big cheering session. Theo said they'd all get bonuses that month, and their shouts of excitement really went through the roof.

"And I'm catering lunch tomorrow," he said. "For everyone." To feed four hundred people took some serious planning, and he ended up spending the afternoon calling across the ocean to four different places to get the job done.

He didn't care. He wanted his employees to know he valued them and the work they did for his companies. Happy employees meant less turnover and better production, and whatever Theo needed to do to make that happen, he'd do it.

He celebrated with his Nine-0 Club on Thursday, and he kissed Katie like he was a dying man on Friday during lunch.

"You're happy today," she said.

"Yeah." He grinned at her, not caring about the food in front of him. "What are you guys doing this weekend?" Theo actually had to work—he had a feeling most of his weekends for the foreseeable future would be filled with coding and meetings and more—but he wanted to pretend like he didn't for a few more minutes.

"I don't know," she said. "I try not to plan too far in advance."

"What?" he asked. "That doesn't sound like you."

She gave him a look that told him he didn't know her well enough to make judgments like that. "Well, since I started Clean Sweep, which has to be so scheduled and regimented, it's nice to not be like that on the weekends."

"Ah, got it."

"Aren't you working?" she asked.

"Well, yeah," he said, ducking his head. "But I was hoping maybe I'd be able to sneak away and see you at some point."

"Sunday's probably the best day. Heather wants to go pick pomegranates tomorrow, and I told her I'd take her. Claire's coming too."

"Claire?"

"She's my best friend," Katie said. "Cleans for me on Saturdays. I clean for her on Wednesdays."

"Wait." Theo looked at her, feeling something sparkling and wonderful between them. "You two clean each other's houses?"

"Yes," Katie said, grinning at him. "I don't like to clean up my own messes. Plus, then my house is clean for the weekend."

"That's so interesting," he said.

"She works for me too," she said. "She's actually more of a partner than just a maid."

"Ah, that's what Ben is for me."

"How come I've never heard about this Ben before?" she asked playfully, and Theo laughed.

"He has a key to my place and everything," he said, reaching for his soda.

"Are you trying to make me jealous?" Katie laughed, and Theo had once thought his life couldn't get any better. The financial success he wanted. The tropical paradise. The club full of men as motivated and as smart as him.

But sitting across from Katie at a simple, outdoor picnic table had added an unforeseen amount of joy to his life.

His phone chimed, signaling the end of their lunch. "I have to go," he said, rising. "I'd love to meet Claire sometime." Again, Theo wasn't a brain surgeon, but he knew best friends had opinions, and he knew Katie would listen to whatever Claire told her.

"Too bad she has a boyfriend," she said, collecting her trash and standing too. "Or maybe she and Ben would like to double with us."

"Ben would like that, even if she does have a boyfriend," Theo said, and they laughed again. He stepped beside her and swept one hand around her waist. He looked down at her, wanting to lay everything he felt out before her. At the same time, he thought it was probably way too early for that.

So he just said, "I sure like spending time with you, Katie," and kissed her until she pulled away.

She ducked her head, licked her lips, and smiled. "See you later, Theo."

He walked away from her then, thinking he'd just fallen in love with her all over again. And he was surprisingly okay with that.

THIRTEEN

KATIE LAY DOWN EVERY NIGHT, congratulating herself on keeping all the balls in the air for another day. Her maids, her daughter, her friends, her yard, and Theo. It was exhausting compartmentalizing everything, but it was a skill she'd learned a long time ago that had helped her from becoming overwhelmed if someone happened to call when she wasn't expecting it.

Of course, those phone calls were usually from the fourth district court in Kansas, and she'd been justified in breaking down, changing into sweats, and staring at the TV for hours on end.

Theo's workload increased, and she saw him a couple of times a week for lunch, and almost every Sunday. October turned the weather a bit cooler, and as the month faded into November, Katie started to make Thanksgiving plans. She normally hosted a small dinner for a few people from Clean Sweep who didn't have any family in the area, a tradition she enjoyed.

As she put out the email to get an idea of how many people she'd need to cook for that year, she thought about Theo and Ben. Maybe they'd like to come too. So she messaged him too, still using the GBS app. It was where they'd first started communicating, and it felt familiar to talk to him there though they texted and spoke on the phone too.

Sure, he said. *I'm in. I'll talk to Ben.*

She still hadn't met Theo's partner yet, but she wasn't in any hurry. Heather seemed to get along great with Theo, and Katie was grateful for that. But she wasn't in a rush to get to a wedding, thinking she should see if his affection and her attraction to him had more staying power than a couple of months.

He never said another word about her website or app, and she felt bad bringing it up when he had two very large, very able-to-pay customers. At the same time, he'd promised her he had time to work on it. But her old systems were still working fine, and she and Theo were getting along so well, she didn't want to say anything.

Another couple of weeks passed, and instead of going out on Sundays, Theo had come over to her house for two Sundays in a row. Before he left, he kissed her so completely Katie wasn't sure how she'd made it through the week before he'd come back into her life.

"Oh, I'm ready to talk about your app," he said when he was halfway out the door. "What's your schedule like this week?"

"Insane," she said. "Everyone wants their house clean for the holidays when their families come over."

"We probably only need a couple of hours," he said. "Mornings are best for me. It's when I do most of my administrative stuff."

She wasn't sure why her app and website had been labeled as his administrative stuff, but she had no idea what he did at work each day.

"I could do Wednesday," she said, thinking she could get Claire's house cleaned in the evening instead of before lunch.

"Great." He grinned at her, that bone-melting grin that made her sag against the wall where she stood. "Nine o'clock?"

"Sure, see you then."

He turned to go, then turned around and came back over to her. She fitted herself right into his arms and received his kiss willingly, feeling herself lose another piece of her heart to him. Again. If she wasn't careful, she'd give him the whole thing again and hope he didn't crush it like he had last time.

She pulled away, and he tucked her hair, whispered, "I love seeing you," and left.

She took out the word "seeing" and let the words play through her mind on a constant loop.

Dangerous, she knew. But she didn't know how to stop this relationship train now. It seemed to have a life of its own, and it was untamed and ferocious and all she could do was hold on and hope she didn't get bucked off.

On Wednesday morning, she didn't dress in her usually cleaning clothes, but took extra time with her hair, makeup, and clothing. She actually put on a skirt—only one of two she actually owned—and added more blush to her cheeks than scrubbing toilets required.

She drove down to the town center of Getaway Bay and navigated over to the Ohana Resort and Condos. The family really had done a great job on all the renovations, and while she'd never been inside one of the luxury units, a couple of her maids had and the reports were impressive.

"What unit?" someone asked her through a speaker, and she fumbled for her phone.

"Um," she said. "I have it here." Theo had texted the unit number to her, as well as directions for where to park. She'd been grateful for those, as the garages here all had numbers, and she wasn't sure if she was supposed to part down the street or not.

"1604," she said into the speaker, almost yelling. Foolishness rushed through her, and she glanced around for a security camera. Of course there would be one, and someone in a dark room somewhere was probably laughing at her.

"Singles Network?" the man asked.

"That's right," she said. "Theodore Fleming."

"Elevator six," he said, and the door clicked, indicating it had been unlocked.

Katie lunged toward it, hoping she wouldn't have to have another embarrassing conversation with a faceless intercom. Thankfully, the elevators were straight ahead, and they had very prominent numbers above them.

She pushed the button for number six and heard a faint whirring sound. Just to see what happened, she pushed the button for another car, but the light didn't brighten. So interesting. She wondered how much someone got paid to talk to people through the speaker and activate elevators.

The elevator dinged and she got on it, her heart racing. Why, she wasn't sure. Only that she'd never been to Theo's office before. Nor his house. He always came to hers. She thought of the first time he'd come and how nervous she'd been. Maybe he as just as anxious as she was.

The elevator came to a smooth stop on the sixteenth floor and she stepped into a silent hallway and faced a sign that indicated there were only four units on this floor. She followed the arrow pointing her toward Theo's and she arrived several moments later.

She wasn't sure if she was supposed to knock or simply go in, the way she would the grocery store. She ended up doing a combination of both, knocking while she pushed open the door. "Hello?"

No one answered her. In fact, there were no lights on and the place had a general feel that no one had been here in hours.

"Theo?" she tried again, but he didn't answer.

This place looked like a condo, with a decorative table by the front door. Everything inside was obviously made of the finest materials available, from bamboo floors to gorgeous curtains billowing gently way down at the windows in front of her.

She walked that way, noting that the air held the slight scent of burnt coffee and that someone had taken great care in selecting and purchasing art for the walls and fancy glass-topped coffee tables.

But there were no dishes anywhere. No errant mugs left behind after a morning meeting. In fact, when she checked, she didn't even find any trash in the can in the kitchen.

"So no one's been here in a while," she said out loud, almost cringing at the sound of her voice in this silent space. Or maybe Theo and Ben simply didn't eat here.

She didn't know. What she did know was that Theo was not here for their nine o'clock meeting.

The place had a pair of black leather couches that felt like they were made of goose feathers when Katie sank onto one. She sighed, put her purse beside her, and waited.

Ten minutes later, she was annoyed.

Twenty minutes passed, and she'd texted Theo three times. He hadn't returned her messages at all. And sometimes he seemed to know what she was going to ask and when before she even started typing.

When a half an hour had gone by, she started to worry. Maybe something had happened to him. Maybe Ben, who she still had never met, had rushed him to the hospital in the back of one of his luxury sports cars.

Surely he'd call any moment. Let her know he was safe, and then he'd apologize and say he was just running late.

No messages through GBS, no texts, and no calls came in. She checked her phone to make sure she had service.

After an hour, Katie got up to leave. She didn't have

time for a two-hour meeting now. She hadn't gotten the time wrong, and she was tired of wasting her time. If there was one thing she absolutely didn't have any to spare, it was time. She felt like she was dealing with Mrs. Chu, and she honestly deserved more respect than that—from both her client and Theo.

At least Mrs. Chu was paying her.

"Theo's doing you a favor," she muttered as she walked toward the exit. Which was true. But her time still meant something to her, and if she hurried, she could get through a lot of the chores at Claire's before she had to be at her next job.

She almost expected to run into Theo in the hallway or the elevator, but she made it all the way back to the lobby of the building without encountering a single soul. She drove much faster over to Claire's, thinking she'd rummage through her friend's closet for something to wear to clean in, because she was severely overdressed to vacuum and mop.

Her anger turned to sadness somewhere along the drive from Theo's condo to Claire's bungalow. When she pulled into the driveway and saw Claire's beat up, white car there, tears pricked her eyes.

She got out and went up the steps to the front door, opening it at the same time she called, "Claire?" just like she had at Theo's.

Footsteps sounded on Claire's non-bamboo floors, and she appeared at the end of the hall, wearing a pair of yellow cleaning gloves. "What are you doing here?" she asked, striding forward. Her eyes broadcasted her worry, and she walked faster when Katie just shook her head.

She finally managed to push out the words, "I came to clean. Why are you doing it?"

"I figured I could do my own for a week," she said. "Jamie canceled *again*."

Katie seized onto the information, because it was something she could deal with. A concrete problem that she could solve. "We need to put her on a sub route," she said. "I'll assign you one of our regulars and put her with Rhonda. She likes to have time off."

Claire nodded, a soft smile touching her lips. "I think she actually encourages her clients to cancel."

Katie gave half a laugh. "Probably."

"Why do you look like someone just told you you'd have to eat pumpkin pie for every meal?"

Katie's tears made an instant reappearance. Only Claire knew her so well. "Theo didn't show up for our meeting."

"Oh, no." Claire stripped the gloves off her hands and put one arm around Katie. "Come on, I'll make apple cider."

"Ew, no," Katie said, but she stepped with Claire, and they walked down the hall and into the kitchen.

"Tell me what happened." Claire moved around the spotless kitchen, and a twinge of guilt stabbed Katie right beneath her ribs.

"You really didn't have to clean," she said. "I was going to bring Heather and start teaching her a few things."

"It's fine," Claire said. "Theo?"

And Katie knew she wouldn't let it drop. "Just what I said. He didn't show up. Didn't call. Didn't text. Nothing."

"Do you think he's okay?"

"If he is, he won't be after I talk to him."

Claire flashed her a smile, but Katie wasn't joking. "Maybe he got the day wrong."

"Maybe."

"Did you try calling his business number?"

"Why would I do that? I was sitting in his office."

"Maybe he thought you were coming to his apartment."

"Then why didn't he pick up the phone when I called him? Three times, Claire." Katie wanted to be mad; it actually felt good. Because now she knew Theo wasn't perfect. Everything had been so rosy and wonderful between them, and Katie knew that kind of romance simply wasn't real.

She didn't need Theo to be bad at something; she just needed him to not be so darn good at everything. And what he was now that he'd ghosted her, she wasn't sure. But it wasn't perfect, and she couldn't believe it, but she actually liked him more because of that.

She sighed, some of the fight leaving her body. "Do you think I should call the cops?"

Her phone rang before Claire could answer, and she flinched. Then she scrambled to get it out of her purse, hoping with everything in her that it was Theo.

"It's him," she said, seeing his name on the screen.

"At least he's not dead," Claire called after her as she headed for the front porch.

"Hey," she said, nowhere near as friendly or flirty as she usually did. "Where are you?"

"Are we not meeting today?" he asked in response.

"I waited for you for an hour," she said.

Silence came through the line, and she gave him the time he needed to come up with the apology. "I thought we were meeting at ten," he said instead.

"No," she said. "Nine." And besides it was almost ten-thirty. He'd waited a half an hour to call her? "I rearranged my whole schedule to meet with you this morning."

"I guess I got the time wrong."

Obviously. "Look, I know you're really busy. You don't need to worry about my website or app. When I'm ready, I'll hire someone."

"What? No, I've got the file right here." He sounded extremely distracted, as he said something to someone obviously in the room with him. Probably Ben.

"I'm thinking of moving back to Kansas," she said.

Four heartbeats of silence came through the line before he said, "Okay, but let's reschedule."

"Sure, yeah," she said, her heart dropping all the way to her toes.

"Great, I'll see you later." The call ended, and Katie watched in disbelief as her screen darkened. He hadn't heard a word she'd said.

She stood, her fury back with a vengeance. Not only that, but she remembered all of the reasons she'd broken up with Theo in the first place. The man worked too much —and he liked it. And these businesses were actually profitable, so there was no way she'd come between him and them.

And Heather?

How could she subject Heather to a man like Theo? Someone who would choose work over her every time?

She couldn't.

She went back inside Claire's house, gripping her phone with too much force. "Hey, I have to go," she called, especially glad she didn't have time to stay and chat when she caught the scent of warming apple cider. How anyone drank that stuff, she'd never understand.

"What did he say?" Claire came out of the kitchen again, this time with a mug clasped in her hands.

"Nothing. I have to go." She flashed a smile. "I owe you big time for doing your own cleaning."

"That's right, you do." Claire gave her a wide smile, and Katie got out of there before her best friend could see that she really wasn't okay, and that Theo had really said nothing. Absolutely nothing.

FOURTEEN

THEO STARED AT HIS PHONE, perplexed and a little annoyed. Why hadn't Katie answered him? For three days now, all of his messages, no matter how he sent them, had gone into a void where she wasn't responding.

He needed to call her. Their missed meeting on Wednesday had likely upset her, though Theo couldn't even really remember what had happened this past week. Everything had been a blur since the phone call from Dallas on Monday about one of their leading metropolitan areas getting reports of abuse through the singles app.

Theo's phone rang before he could move a muscle toward it, but it wasn't Katie. "Hey, Ben," he said after swiping open the call. He almost didn't want to ask. "What's up?"

Noon had just come and gone on Saturday, and Theo was hoping for a nap. Then maybe he'd go figure out what he'd done wrong with Katie and make it right.

"Boston PD would like an official statement," he said. "They're holding their statement until they have your statement."

Theo looked at the email he'd been composing for the last hour. It only had one sentence in it. "I'm working on it," he said.

"I'll be up in a minute." The line went dead, and Theo exhaled heavily as he set his phone back on his desk.

His official statement was that he wasn't responsible for how people used their apps. Of course there would be people posing as something and someone they weren't. They'd been doing that online for decades.

But he thought of the ride share fiasco, and he knew he'd have to put out a strong statement that showed his disapproval of any type of sexual misconduct or abuse through the use of his app.

He frowned at his computer screen and started typing.

"Let me see it," Ben said as he walked through the door. He wore full business attire as if it was normal for him to dress in such a way on Saturdays. Theo couldn't remember the last time he'd had a shower, let alone a full meal.

Ben set a pastry box on the desk. "Eat something while I look at it." He came around the desk, and Theo got up and switched him places.

"Did you bring coffee?"

"Did you see me carrying coffee?" Ben threw him a glance, and the statement summed up the stress level for both of them.

"Sorry," Theo mumbled, slouching in his chair and ignoring the doughnuts.

"This is good," Ben said a moment later. He tapped, backspaced, and typed something else in. "I'm sending it."

"Go ahead." Theo would read it about fifty times in the dozens of articles that were sure to come out over the next couple of days. "Have you heard anything else from the police department?"

"They said they'd call you once they had the statement. Then we'll get the whole file, and someone will go over it with us."

"Then we'll know what we're dealing with," Theo said.

"This might cost some money, Theo."

"I'm aware." He closed his eyes and rubbed his forehead, where a headache had been plaguing him for six straight days. "I looked up that thing with the ride sharing." He opened his eyes and looked at Ben. "What did legal say? Our language is compliant?"

"One hundred percent," Ben said. "We could fight any litigation that comes and have grounds."

"We'll wait and see." Theo reached for the doughnut box. "Maybe this story will just splash all over the front pages for a few days and then be done."

Ben looked at Theo's computer screen. "They've responded already."

Theo practically launched himself out of his chair and around the desk so he could see the email. "Open it."

Ben clicked, and the words came up. He read out loud, "Thank you for this statement. We're going to release it at seven p.m. Eastern time today, and I'd like to talk to you before then. Is now a good time to call?"

Theo's phone chimed at the same time he said, "Tell him yes, please call." He looked at his phone. "Oh, this is him, asking the same thing. I'll text him."

He tapped out a quick text that said, *Call anytime,* and looked at his best friend. "Here we go."

Sure enough, a moment later, his phone rang, and Theo swiped open the call from the Chief of Police in Boston. "Hello, Chief Wisehour," he said. "Can I put you on speaker so my partner can hear everything?"

"Sure," the other man said. "You're in a conference with me, my secretary Monica, and my first Lieutenant, Bryce Watson."

Watson was the man who had first alerted Theo to a problem, six days ago. "Great," he said, switching the call to speaker. "It's me here, and Ben Brown, the second-in-command at Singles Network."

Their eyes met, and Theo felt as much worry cascading through him as he saw in Ben's expression. His stomach flipped, and he pressed his eyes closed in a long blink.

"Monica is sending the file to your email address now," Chief Wisehour said. "No charges have been filed, so I want to be clear about that. I, nor is anyone on this call, am not a lawyer. We're recording the call."

Theo nodded to Ben, who reached for the cord and plugged it into Theo's phone. "We are too, so we can send it to our legal team in Dallas."

No charges have been filed rang through his head. So far, so good. "So tell us, Chief. What's the exact complaint?"

"A woman came in and said she'd been assaulted on a date with a man she'd met through Boston People & Singles, or BPS. Our initial officer was Sergeant Bethany Howser, and the case was quickly moved over to our sexual crimes unit."

Theo swallowed, wishing he had something nearby to drink. Something to fiddle with. Something to get this nervous energy out of his system.

"It turns out, however, that after questioning the victim, as well as the accused, and a few other people— they're all in the report—there was no assault that happened. A better term would be 'taken advantage of.'"

Theo watched the computer screen and nodded toward it as another message appeared at the top. "We just got the case file," he said. "And what does 'taken advantage of' mean?"

"Quite simply, she was robbed," the Chief said. "She met a man for coffee—a man she met through your app— and according to witnesses, he did yell at her for a few minutes. Then he got up and left, apparently with all of her cash and credit cards."

Ben had the file open and the printer started whirring. "Printing it," he said softly.

"So does my statement fit with a robbery?" Theo asked. "I thought we were dealing with something of a sexual nature."

"I thought so too," the Chief said. "I still think your statement fits. You don't condone any use of the app where someone is dishonest or uses it to meet people with the intent to commit a crime."

Theo started nodding, glad Ben had been able to make that clear in the mess Theo had started. "That's right. Honestly, Chief, I'm not sure what else we need to do."

"Well, right now, nothing. We'll put the statement out. You understand why we have to. Social media and app abuse is a hot button topic, and we feel it's better to address it than let the public speculate."

"I understand."

"We give no details on active cases," the other man, Bryce Watson, said. "So all our statement will be is that we have received the complaint and are following up with all witnesses and leads. Then we'll say we've reached out to you and read your statement. There will be no questions. It will last probably thirty seconds."

Thirty seconds. Theo could weather thirty seconds of bad publicity. He hoped. He'd actually had businesses fail with less than that. He pushed those thoughts away, choosing instead to focus on this problem. Here, now.

"Will it be aired online?" Ben asked. "We'd like to watch it."

"We've invited all the major news networks," the Chief said. "It starts in twenty minutes."

Ben stood and headed for the door, probably to go get the TV on so he could find a news channel broadcasting out of Boston. "Okay," Theo said. "We'll find it." It wouldn't be hard after the story hit the air. Then all the Internet news websites would have it up too. Heck, Theo could probably get on Facebook and find the video only seconds after it went live.

"Thank you for responding so readily to our requests," the Chief said. "We'll be in touch."

"Thank you," Theo said, and the call ended. He collapsed in his desk chair, utterly drained. He just needed a few seconds to think, to figure things out. But his mental energy seemed to be completely gone.

"Theo," Ben called from the other room, and up Theo got. He found his friend standing in front of the huge television in the living area of the condo—the reception area if clients ever came—the clicker in his hand.

"CNN has it on the ticker at the bottom of the screen. They'll be cutting to a live feed of it at the top of the hour."

"Great," Theo said, though it felt anything but great. "I have time to go get coffee, don't I?"

Ben looked at him like he'd gone off the deep end. "I guess."

"Be back then." Theo swiped his keys off the kitchen counter and almost ran from the office. He didn't go down to the beach and make the two-block walk to Roasted like he'd done many times over the months he'd been in Getaway Bay.

Instead, he took the stairs up one floor to his house and set a pot of coffee to brew in his kitchen. His place didn't hold much more comfort or the feel of home than the office did, but he was finally able to breathe.

And after he did that, with the room filling with the scent of liquid caffeine that he desperately needed, he called Katie again.

"Please pick up," he muttered to him. "Please, please

pick up." For some reason he wanted to talk to her before the story hit the public headlines.

Just when he thought the line was going to go to voicemail, she said, "Hello?" as if she didn't know it would be him on the other end of the line.

"Katie," he said, relief painting all the letters in her name. "I know we have a lot to talk about, and I want to do that. But I just want you to know that...." He wasn't sure how to phrase it. "My Singles Network has come under scrutiny in Boston. There will be a live public announcement about it at one. Like, in fifteen minutes. And...and...and I guess I wanted you to know."

He wanted her there at his side, reassuring him that everything would be okay. He wanted her there at his side, so he could hold onto her and steal her comfort and safety. He wanted her there at his side, because that was where she belonged and he needed her to do hard things.

And this was a very hard thing for him.

"Oh," she said, pure surprise in her voice. "I wasn't expecting any of that."

"I know," he said. "That's why I wanted to talk to you. I'm so glad you answered this time." He wasn't accusing her of anything, but he realized how his sentence sounded after he'd said it. "Anyway, can I maybe stop by later and tell you more?"

"Yes," she said quietly, and more relief than Theo had ever felt moved through him. "We're not going anywhere today."

"Great," he said, feeling like he could end the call with

I love you and be speaking the truth. Instead, he said, "I'll be in touch."

With his coffee brewed and full of sugar, he headed back upstairs with five minutes to spare before the announcement, hoping he wasn't about to lose everything in a thirty-second press conference.

FIFTEEN

KATIE SAT ON THE COUCH, looking at Theo's handsome face and silver hair in a photo as the reporter talked about him. It felt surreal to hear his name and what he'd accomplished from the television when she knew so much more of the man behind the app, behind the face.

She exhaled, and her breath came out shaky, testifying of her nerves. Claire sat right beside her, and her hand around Katie's tightened.

"Let's go live to Boston now," the female reporter said. "Where the Chief of Police, Lars Wisehour, is ready with a statement."

A burly, broad-shouldered man who looked like he'd dealt with more than his fair share of criminals filled the screen. He wore his full uniform, the hat included, and looked directly at the camera with his dark brown eyes.

"Good evening," he said. "On behalf of the entire police department here in Boston, we want everyone to know that we take every complaint brought to our officers very seriously. We have an entire unit devoted to Internet and web-based crimes, and we follow every lead until an appropriate decision can be made. Several days ago, on Monday, November twelfth, a complaint was logged about an assault. We will not give the details of any open case, but we quickly learned that this alleged assault happened as a result of two people of appropriate age using an app called Boston People & Singles."

He paused and looked down at the podium. A moment later, he focused on the crowd again. "We're currently in the course of investigating and expect all citizens to cooperate fully. We contacted the developer of the app and have a statement from Theodore Fleming, who currently resides in Getaway Bay, Hawaii." He cleared his throat and looked to his side, then stepped away from the mic so another tall, wide man could take his place.

"Good evening," he said, purely professional. Katie wondered if police officers had to take public relations courses. "This is the statement we received from Mister Fleming, less than an hour ago." He lifted a paper but didn't really look at it before starting to speak again.

"Singles Network and any of its variations have never condoned or encouraged inappropriate behavior by any user. Those who choose to use the app should understand that it only operates based on what it's given, and that other users could potentially lie about who they are, where they live, how old they are, or any number of other items. Singles Network hopes, encourages, and has warning statements at the signup of the app that all users will be honest in all things, and use the app for its true purpose: to find a relationship worth living in for the rest of your life. Any use of the app for anything other than that, or to commit any type of crime, is illegal and will not be tolerated by our company or police departments across the globe. We express our condolences in this case and hope a resolution can be reached without further damage to any party."

The man stopped talking, and Katie realized she hadn't blinked in quite a long time. "That sounded so official."

"So smart," Claire agreed.

"Thank you," the man said. "There will be no questions, as this is an active case."

Reporters began to shout anyway, and the feed continued as the female reporter started talking over the video. "Theodore Fleming, owner and CEO of Singles Network, as well as two other web development companies, is said to be worth eight-point-two billion dollars, and his popular app bringing people and places together to make a love connection is used in two hundred and four cities across the country, by over twelve million people."

Claire said, "Wow. This could be bad for him."

Katie's insides felt like someone had encased them in gelatin and then kept flicking them, making them quake and shake. "He's coming over later." Her voice sounded like she'd swallowed something too big and had scraped her throat. "I feel so bad for him."

"Eight-point-two billion dollars," Claire said. "What does that much money even look like?"

Katie swung her head toward her best friend, who

clicked off the TV before meeting Katie's eye. She dissolved into giggles, and Katie couldn't help joining her. She wasn't happily laughing, but it did release some of her pent-up nerves.

"I haven't been responding to him," she said, sudden guilt gutting her. "He's called and texted a bunch of times since Wednesday."

"You've always been so stubborn." Claire stood up. "Does he have any brothers? Friends?"

Katie got up and followed her into the kitchen. "What about you and Chuck?"

"He seems to care more about deep sea fishing than me." Claire shrugged, but her eyes were bright and a bit nervous. "Or he's at work. It just...it wasn't working. I broke up with him last night."

"Oh, honey." Katie went around the counter and wrapped her friend in a hug. "Why didn't you say something?"

"Oh, you know." Claire sniffed and held on tight to Katie's shoulders. "I feel kind of stupid. We've been together for a long time, and I guess I just thought maybe we'd get back together."

"Do you want to get back together with Chuck?"

Claire thought about it for a moment. "No. Not really."

"Well, Theo does have a friend. His name's Ben, and I guess he's like CEO number two or something."

"What does he look like?"

"I haven't met him." Katie opened the fridge though she wasn't hungry. She closed it again and got out ice cream. "This is what we need. Then we can plot how I'm going to deal with Theo tonight, and how you're going to charm Ben until he walks you down the aisle."

Claire rolled her eyes, but Katie got out two spoons and handed on to her friend. Nothing was established, though, except the fact that she ate more calories in that hour than she had all week.

When Theo texted to ask if now was a good time for him to come, Katie still had no solutions for her feelings. And when he showed up on her front porch and Heather launched herself at him and hugged him around the waist for a full minute, Katie simply watched, knowing if things didn't work out with Theo, she'd be dealing with two broken hearts.

"I have a painting in an art show soon," Heather said, looking up at him. "Will you come?"

"Yeah, sure," he said, grinning down at her.

She ran off with, "Thanks, Theo! I'm going to watch videos in my room."

"Hey," he said once he and Katie were alone. He looked exhausted, his suit more rumpled than usual, and a lock of hair completely out of place.

"Come in," Katie said. "When's the last time you ate?"

"I don't know, honestly." He stepped into her house, and then right into her arms. "I've missed you so much," he said into her neck, and she simply held him for a few moments.

She stepped back and cleared her throat. "Well, we ordered pizza tonight, and there's plenty still sitting on the counter." She led the way down the hall and sat at the bar with him while he picked up four slices of pizza.

He ate through one before asking, "Did you watch it?"

"Yes," she said.

"No charges have been filed," he said. "Maybe nothing else will come of it. How was our statement?"

"Brilliant," she said. "Very official."

"Thanks. I wrote some of it. Ben polished it up."

Katie thought about mentioning Claire but decided it wasn't a good time. She just nodded while he took another bite of pizza.

When the tension between them felt like it might break, she said, "I'm sorry I haven't been responding. I...I got my feelings hurt when you didn't show up for our meeting."

He swung his attention toward her. "Is that what it was? I've been racking my brain all week, trying to figure out what I did wrong."

"I don't think you have time to work on my website and app."

He sighed, regret filling those beautiful eyes. "I probably don't."

"Then *don't*," she said. "And just say so. I asked you a bunch of times. You said it was okay."

"I'm sorry," he said, the apology she'd wanted on Wednesday finally coming out. "I should've said so. Things just got messed up this week, and...." He gazed at her, tipping forward. "I'm sorry." His last apology came out in a whisper, and it completely melted Katie's heart.

She leaned forward to close the distance between them, giving him a quick kiss. "Okay, so, are you too busy to come to Thanksgiving dinner next week?"

"No, of course not."

"You're sure?"

"Katie, it's Thanksgiving." He looked at her, those blue eyes firing with emotion now. "I'll be here. Ben will be here. He's even bringing that potato casserole of his mother's."

"Okay," she said, wanting to put all her faith and trust in the two of them. "We're eating at one o'clock. Come any time."

"What's Heather making?"

"The mashed potatoes and gravy," Katie said, glad they'd moved on to a safer conversation topic. "And the yams. Claire's making the rolls. I'm doing the turkey— very American, I know. And one of my ladies is bringing some traditional Hawaiian poi and poke. And another one is bringing sushi as an appetizer."

"How many of us will be there?"

"Uh, Claire just broke up with Chuck, so he's not coming. Opens the door for Ben," Katie sing-songed and nudged Theo, who finally smiled like he was alive. "Eight, I think. Me and Heather. You and Ben. Claire. And three ladies from work: Rhonda, Cicily, and Lace."

"Sounds nice," he said, and he left the rest of his pizza on the counter and headed for the back door. She went with him, glancing behind her as she left the house to make sure Heather wasn't following. She'd gone into her bedroom when Theo had opted for the pizza.

She sat with Theo in the swing, feeling cherished when he laid his head on her shoulder and fell asleep. It was the perfect evening, with the almost-perfect man, and Katie was glad she'd confessed to him why she'd gone silent.

Now she could focus on the upcoming meal and making sure everyone had a good Thanksgiving.

———

The timer went off on the oven, indicating the rolls were done. "Can you grab that?" Heather asked, shifting to the side so Katie could open the oven and she could keep whisking the gravy. "This is almost done, and I don't want it to burn."

Katie pulled the rolls out and set them on a couple of counter savers on the island. "Claire, you can butter these."

Everyone had arrived for the feast and now it was just a matter of getting all the pieces in place. Theo had carved the turkey, and it waited covered with aluminum foil, for everything else to be finished.

The sushi appetizers had been a big hit—not with Katie, as she didn't particularly enjoy raw fish, but with everyone else. Theo and Ben had arrived about ten, and Ben and Claire had been making eyes at each other for hours.

Katie wouldn't be surprised if her best friend got the man's number before the day was over, and a rush of gratitude for her life and happiness that she could afford to have people over for this meal had been surging all morning.

"Yams are done," she said, ticking things off on her fingers. "Rolls, potatoes, turkey, the casserole Ben brought, poke, poi, and the salad." She turned back to the stove, where four dirty pots were stacked. "We're just waiting on the gravy."

"It's done," Heather announced, and she moved the gravy boat closer to the stove. "I need you to pour it."

Katie did, then put it on the counter with all the other food, grabbed a plate with butter on it, and put the salt and pepper shakers beside all of that. "Okay," she called. "We're ready. Can someone go grab the people outside?"

Cicily moved over to the door and motioned for those that had gone out there to come in. Theo, Ben, Lace, and Rhonda squeezed their way inside, and Katie's eyes caught on Theo's. She'd never in a million years thought she'd be celebrating another holiday with him. Thought that opportunity had sailed many years ago.

He smiled at her, seemingly thinking the same thing, and tucked his hands in his pockets. He wore a pair of khaki shorts and a festive, pumpkin-colored polo, making himself look relaxed and delicious at the same time.

"Okay," she said, pulling her gaze from him. "Thank you all for coming. It's so good to have you here." Her voice caught on the last word. "I know what it's like to be far from family at special times, and I just want you to know I think of all of you as family." She looked at every one of them, even Ben who she'd just met hours before.

She could see why he and Theo got along so well. Ben had a quick smile and he'd obviously interacted with a lot of people in his lifetime. He was much younger than Theo, and Theo claimed he kept him relevant.

How much younger? Katie had been allowed to text Theo while he stood five feet from her, and he'd said Ben was thirty-four. Katie had spent the next couple of hours while bread rose and turkey roasted whispering to Claire every time she passed her that forty-one was not too old for a thirty-four-year-old boyfriend.

Lace had agreed, and she'd promised she'd start feeling Ben out to see if he was looking for a date.

"Claire is going to say grace," Katie said. "And then I'll go over the food." She folded her arms and smiled at Heather as her daughter stepped beside her. Claire said a beautiful prayer of thanksgiving, and then Katie pointed to the end of the counter.

"Take whatever you want. There's a big table outside, and we can all fit there." She smiled. "The turkey was stuffed with sausage stuffing, and that's here." She pointed to the mixture Lace had brought over early that morning and helped her stuff into the bird before Katie had slid it into the oven. "And there's cans of soda in the cooler on the deck. And bottles of lemonade. And a big jug of ice water." She beamed around at everyone, glad they'd gotten all the details done and it was barely after one o'clock.

"All right," she said when no one moved. "Don't be shy."

Lace walked forward with, "I'm starving, I'll go first," which broke the ice. Everyone fell into line after that, and Katie stayed back to watch them. She twisted into Theo's body when he put his arm around her, and she went with him when it was finally their turn to get food.

"This all looks great," he said. "Last year, I ate at the Sweet Breeze buffet."

"Oh, I've heard of that," Katie said. "Is it good?"

"Yeah, it was really great." Theo glanced at her for a long moment, clearly deciding something. "I'm friends with the owner. They let me sit with their family."

Of course he knew Fisher DuPont. It seemed the man was surrounded by wealth at every turn, and besides, everyone in Getaway Bay knew who Fisher was. He'd come to Getaway Bay about six years ago and completely transformed the tourist industry. More people on the island meant the economy stayed up, and a lot of people had benefitted from his huge resort and spa, even if they'd been concerned about it in the beginning.

"I know his wife," she said, wanting to put in her claim to fame too. "She contracts us to clean her bed and breakfast. I send three ladies there every afternoon." It was actually one of Katie's greatest accomplishments, and she wanted to get into more Mom and Pop businesses like Stacey's.

But her growth had exploded, and she'd barely been able to keep up with the residential work she had.

"Oh, that's great," Theo said. "I should hire you to come clean my place." He chuckled, but Katie seized onto his statement.

"I can do that. The office too. I noticed it had a weird smell when I was there."

Theo paused. "A weird smell?"

Katie giggled at the concerned look on his face. "Yes, sir. You definitely need a maid."

He realized she was teasing him, and he smiled too. "Good thing I know where to find the best maid on the island." He nodded for her to go first through the back door, and she found that Claire had saved two spots for her and Theo right at the end of the table.

Ben sat next to her, and Lace across from her, so the conversation would never stop. Katie felt a rush of affection for her friends as she sat down, giving them both a warm smile she hoped would convey how she felt about them.

"So maybe don't eat that potato casserole," Ben said.

"Why not?" Katie had taken a big scoop of it to show her support. She forked up a bite and put it in her mouth.

"It's so salty," Ben said. "I don't know what I did wrong."

Katie didn't want to spit out the offending food, but it was the saltiest thing she'd ever eaten. She forced herself to swallow it and put a smile on her face. "Seems like maybe you put too much salt in it."

Theo started laughing, and Katie nudged him. "Be nice."

"Dude, you said you could cook." He continued laughing, and when Ben joined in, Katie pushed her casserole to the edge of her plate.

"Claire's good with casseroles," Katie said. "I bet if she looked at the recipe, she could help you with it."

"Funny," Ben said. "Lace said the exact same thing."

"Literally word for word," Lace said, grinning.

Claire's whole face was turning red, and she hid, with her head half-ducked, behind her hair. "You guys are so embarrassing."

"So how about you give me your number?" Lace said,

leaning up onto the table with her elbows, her phone clutched in her hands. "And I'll give it to Claire when you're not around. Then she won't have to be embarrassed."

Katie giggled though Claire looked like she could easily commit homicide right there at the Thanksgiving table.

Ben chuckled, not a flush in sight. "All right. You ready?"

"So ready," Lace said, enjoying herself a little too much in Katie's opinion. But Ben rattled off his number, and Lace grinned at him like they might be going out later. The conversation flowed from there to other things, and Lace asked when Heather's art exhibit would be.

"It's during the Christmas festival," Katie said. "I think it's December ninth to the eleventh. It's just three days." She glanced at Theo. "I think we're going on Friday night."

"Yeah, the first day," he said. "We can't miss Heather's painting."

Warmth filled Katie over and over again until she was sure she could've roasted a turkey with only her body. When dinner was over, she snuggled with Theo in the shade, hopeful that this would be the first of many holidays with him.

SIXTEEN

THEO WORKED NEARLY non-stop for the next couple of weeks. The scandal in Boston had faded, but it hadn't gone away completely. The woman still hadn't filed any charges against Singles Network, but she had pressed charges against the man she'd met for coffee.

Ben kept telling him that that was exactly what she should've done. Held the individual who did the crime responsible. Not the company who'd developed the app. Theo agreed, but he still didn't feel like the situation was resolved.

Things with Katie had improved, but he was so busy he rarely saw her for more than a few hours a week on Sunday afternoon. She didn't seem bothered by the limited attention from him, but of course, he hadn't known why she'd gone dark back when he'd missed their meeting.

He was trying, but there simply weren't enough hours in the day to do everything. He had to eat, shower, work out, make phone calls, send emails, meet with clients, and develop websites and apps. It was difficult to add Katie and Heather to that equation, though they were who he wanted to be spending his mental energy on and his time with.

The Sunday before the Christmas festival, he spent the afternoon helping Heather and Katie decorate their Christmas tree. Heather bubbled on about the festival, and how she couldn't wait to see all the paintings. He learned the festival sort of echoed the State Fair in that ribbons would be awarded in some categories. Baking, quilting, painting, photography, and more. And Heather had entered in both painting and baking.

"What did you make?" he asked her.

"Sourdough bread," she said. "The starter is really tricky."

"I don't even know what that means," he said, glancing at Katie, who seemed to be wearing a perpetual smile today.

"It's the mixture you use to host the yeast," Heather said. "That starter and yeast is what makes the sourdough sour when other breads aren't."

Theo blinked at her. "You win for knowing that," he said.

Heather smiled at him. "My grandma taught me that."

"Oh?" Theo's eyes flew to Katie's, noting that her smile had slipped a bit.

"Yeah, she visited us for a few weeks before we moved here," Heather said as if she hadn't noticed her mother's mood shift. "I text her sometimes to ask questions. Mom says she was a great baker."

"She is," Katie said, hanging another ornament.

Theo kept slipping the hooks through the balls and handing them to Heather to hang. In no time at all, the tree was done, and he stood back with Katie and Heather to admire it. He had a flash of what his future could be, right here in this house, with these two. And he wanted it very much.

They spent the rest of the day curled up inside, something playing on the TV. When it was time for Theo to go, he kissed Katie and hugged Heather, saying, "I'll see you guys on Friday."

The next morning, Ben entered the office with a piece of paper in his hand. "What's that?" Theo asked dubiously. Ben never entered a room empty-handed, but Theo liked the muffins, bagels, or doughnuts he usually brought much better than a piece of paper.

Ben grinned as he set the paper on Theo's desk and slid it toward him. Theo reached between his monitors and brought it closer. "What is this?" He scanned the top of the page, which was their standard pre-signing notice.

"You're joking." His heart started pumping out extra beats, and he sank back in his chair. "You got The Grocery Guys."

"They want an app that includes online ordering as well as delivery options." Ben sat across from him, and Theo pushed down his monitor so he could see over it. "I think we should give it to a different team," he said, turning serious.

"Here?" Theo asked. "Or in Dallas."

"No matter what, it's time to hire more people," Ben said. "They're already drowning in Dallas, and there's no way we can handle Gladstone, Island Airways, and The Grocery Guys."

"Fisher's handy with computer science," Theo mused. "I wonder if he'd know anyone in the Getaway Bay area. We have room here for more people."

"It would be good to expand outside of Texas." Ben shrugged, though he'd said the same thing in the past.

"Let's start that process." Theo pulled out his phone. "I'll text Fisher." Ten minutes later, he had a meeting with the man in his penthouse on the twenty-eighth floor at Sweet Breeze for the following morning.

As Theo approached the door the next day, his nerves made him stop and pull a mint from his pocket. He wasn't sure why he was so nervous to talk to Fisher. He'd known the man for a while, and he'd come to lots of Nine-0 Club meetings over the months he'd been in Getaway Bay.

He knocked and waited, surprised when Fisher himself opened the door wearing a pair of shorts, a T-shirt, and an apron around his waist. "Come in," he said. "I'm trying to feed the baby."

Theo blinked at Fisher's retreating back and then entered the penthouse. This looked like a home, where people lived and enjoyed each other's company. A little boy played in the living room, making noises as he ran a truck along a very expensive-looking couch. "Say hi, Micah."

"Hi," the little boy said.

"And this one." Fisher sighed and looked down at the other child in the highchair. "He's decided he doesn't like vegetables. He's barely one." Fisher took the chair in front of the baby boy and picked up the spoon. "Look, bud, I don't care if you eat them. But it makes Mom happy, okay? So open up."

The boy didn't open his mouth, and Fisher gave up. "Fine. But you're telling her." He stood and went into the kitchen, where he washed his hands and wrung out a washcloth. He cleaned up the baby and got him out of the chair. "Go play."

The baby toddled off, falling after a couple of steps. Theo had no idea what to do with small children—or this version of Fisher.

"So, you need more people?" Fisher asked. "Coding experts?"

"Preferably," Theo said. "We're doing high-end website and app development for big players in their industries. They set the standard. When people see their apps, they want to emulate them."

"Then you want Jack Harper," Fisher said. "He lives up on the bluff, and he's mostly a hacker."

Theo frowned and moved over to the dining room table with Fisher. "A hacker?"

"He's retired from the FBI," Fisher said, pulling out his phone. "Let me text him."

"How do you know him?"

"Oh, Jason does some private contracting with the police sometimes," Fisher said like it was no big deal. "He knew him, and I met him once at a dinner at their house."

"Hm." Theo waited, wondering if that was who he really wanted to build an app for someone who wanted to deliver organic groceries in sixteen cities around the country.

"He says he's coming down to town on Friday." Fisher shook his head and chuckled softly. "He's such a strange guy. Only leaves his house once a week." He glanced up at Theo. "So is Friday okay?"

"Yeah, sure," Theo said. "Wait. What time?"

Fisher glanced up at him. "Jack doesn't schedule times. He shows up when he shows up."

Theo shook his head. "What? Why?"

"He doesn't want anyone to know where he's going to be at a specific time. He rotates which days he comes down to town, never sticking to the same schedule when he does." Fisher started tapping on his phone. "I told you, he's a bit odd."

"But he can work full-time on extravagant apps?" Theo asked. "I don't know, Fisher...."

"Oh, he's glued to the Internet," Fisher said. "And his devices." He turned his phone so Theo could see that Jack had texted Fisher at least four times in the last twenty seconds they'd been talking about the man. "See? He'll get the job done. And he's good."

"Fine, tell him yes." Theo needed someone to get the job done, and he needed someone good. He could still get to the Christmas festival. He could.

———

The hours and days blurred together until Friday arrived, and even then, he was in a mad rush to finish one of the features in the Gladstone app before Lawrence stopped by to see the progress.

Lawrence played with the app, asking questions and requesting new features as well as changes to the ones Theo had already coded. "It's not that simple," he said. "You think I can just put a box there, but that's a whole new level of code."

Lawrence looked at him, his face full of seriousness. "Can you do it?"

"Of course I can do it," Theo said. "But it's a week's worth of work, not something I run in and change few letters around and have you try it while you're here." Most people didn't get that about computer science. They thought it was so simple to add things to forms or options to lists or for just this one thing to appear. But it took new code, testing, trial and error, and sometimes Theo would have to scrap everything he'd done and start over.

"I'm not in a hurry," Lawrence said. "I'd like the option of my business customers to be able to use a regular version of the app."

"No problem," Theo said, glancing at the clock. Jack hadn't shown up yet, and he'd been working with Lawrence for a couple of hours. They finished up shortly after that, and Theo sighed as the office became his again. Ben had taken off early so he could call his mother and then go meet Claire for dinner.

His phone buzzed, and he hoped with everything in him that it was Jack, saying he was on his way up. But it was Fisher, and it was an address. Another message came in that said, *Jack wants you to go up to his place. He didn't come down today after all. Something about someone watching the house.*

Theo didn't hesitate. He grabbed his keys and headed for the door. The Grocery Guys had not officially signed, as they wanted a dedicated team of developers in place before they did. While Lawrence was not in a hurry for his app to be done, The Grocery Guys were. Apparently, their biggest competitor already had an app, and they were playing catch-up.

He drove through downtown, cursing the Friday afternoon traffic. Once he got on the road that led up to the bluffs, things got better, and he pushed his car to several miles above the speed limit. After all, the sooner he got to Jack's, the quicker he could get back.

He pulled in to the specified driveway and peered up at the gate. He couldn't even see a house, so how in the world would someone be watching it? Theo pressed the buzzer and waited.

"Name," someone barked.

He gave his whole name, adding, "Fisher DuPont sent me up to talk to you about app development?"

The gate rumbled open, and it seemed like it needed a new motor, because it took forever. By the time Theo got through and down to the house and up to the front door, at least five minutes had passed.

An older gentleman with white hair opened the door. At least Theo knew what he had to look forward to. "Are you Jack?" he asked.

"Yes." The man glanced over Theo's shoulder. "Come in." He stepped back and Theo entered the house.

Jack did not need a maid, and the fresh scent of lemons hung in the air. "This way." He led Theo to the right and then left down a hall to an office. The room was drenched in darkness, and when Jack shuffled over to the windows and opened the blinds, Theo saw the command center where the man surely spent most of his time.

This room could definitely use a good cleaning, but Theo could appreciate the four screens, two on each side of the luxury desk chair. Three used coffee cups sat on the edge of the desk, behind the monitors, and the books in the built-in shelves were only collecting dust.

"Tell me about your business," Jack said, and Theo had the distinct impression that he was the one giving the interview that day. So he sat in the only other available chair and started talking about the web and app development arm of his company.

"You'd specifically be working with The Grocery Guys," he said, swiping open his phone and pulling up their current website. "They want to add online and mobile ordering, as well as instant delivery options." He passed his phone to the other man. "They need a lot of attention, and they want their app done as soon as possible."

Jack looked at the phone for a few moments, pulling the screen down as he scrolled. "Let me show you something, son." Jack set the phone on his desk and gestured for Theo to come around to the other side.

Son rang through Theo's ears. He was almost fifty years

old, for crying out loud. True, Jack probably had fifteen years on him. Maybe twenty. But son? Still, he obliged without saying anything, and looked at the monitors in front of Jack.

"This is a project I've been working on for a while." Jack launched into a story about a man that he'd spent a decade looking for. He now had websites and databases he cultivated from old FBI files, and every time Theo thought he might be able to interject and say he had to go, Jack would start a new story.

And his phone sat so close and yet so far away. Three feet, on the other side of Jack's body, so Theo couldn't just grab it and text anyone for help.

All he could do was pray that someone, somewhere, would know of his predicament and come save him.

SEVENTEEN

"MOM, we're going to be late." Heather stood at the front door, wearing her bright blue dress, her hair all plaited and ready to go.

"I know." Katie looked at her phone. She'd sent half a dozen messages to Theo, and he hadn't responded once.

"Is he coming?" Heather asked.

Katie couldn't stand to see her daughter disappointed. She'd worked so hard for this night, spending every day after school with Tina as she finished her painting. She'd delivered it on Monday, according to the schedule, and she was practically bursting to find out if she'd earned a ribbon or not.

"Remember that you did your best," Katie said, collecting her keys and purse and starting for the front door too. "You can't control anything other than that."

"I know, Mom." Heather smiled up at her. "Is Theo

coming?" So much anxiety ran through her daughter's expression.

Katie said, "He's going to meet us there." Instant regret stung her lungs, but she couldn't stand to see Heather upset before they'd even gotten to the festival. "Claire and Ben are already there," she added. "And Lace is going tomorrow after her jobs." She put her arm around Heather and opened the front door. "So let's go. I've been ready forever."

"Mom." Heather rolled her eyes and went first down the steps. Katie watched her, offering a silent prayer that she would at least have a third place ribbon. An honorable mention. Something. Anything.

The drive over to the community center seemed to take no time at all, and still Theo hadn't texted. Katie put her arm protectively around Heather as they walked in.

"There she is," Claire said brightly, focusing only on Heather. She hugged her and said, "We waited for you guys, so we haven't seen it yet."

Katie positioned herself next to Ben as they started walking toward the entrance to the exhibits. "Where's Theo?" she hissed through clenched teeth. She could not imagine a single scenario where he would be unable to be here. Not one—unless he'd chosen something else, deemed it more important, over this festival.

But how could he do that when he knew how important it was to Heather?

"I don't know," Ben said. "He had a meeting with someone this afternoon, but it should've ended by now."

He pulled out his phone. "Let me call him." He stepped away, and Katie fell back too.

"Just a minute," she called to Claire and Heather, and they turned back to her. "Ben's calling Theo." Her blood boiled through her veins, and it was so uncomfortable Katie wanted to scream. Anger, bitterness, frustration, and anxiety frothed together, making a very big mess inside her.

"He's not answering," Ben said. "Which is so unusual. Something must be wrong."

Katie could only nod. "Well, we've waited long enough." He was supposed to meet them at their house thirty minutes ago, and with the drive, he was easily forty-five minutes late. "Let's go."

"But I want Theo to see it," Heather whined, already the beginning of her breakdown happening.

"The festival goes for two more days, hon," Claire said. "Come on. Let's go see it. Don't you want to see if you got a ribbon?" She looked at Katie, who mouthed a silent *Thank you*, and got Heather moving toward the entrance.

They wandered the quilts, pointing out the intricate patterns in the winning creation. Onto the baked goods, and Heather had a bright white ribbon on her loaf of sour-dough bread.

"Second place," she said, turning back to Heather with a big, beaming smile on her face.

"That's great, bug." Katie gave her a high-five, and so did Claire and Ben.

"Look, that peach pie won." Heather stood in front of it

for a few minutes—long enough to make Katie wonder what she could possibly be thinking.

"The art is next," she said, prompting Heather to move. She did, but she'd fallen really quiet, and she held her right hand in a fist. "Relax." Katie reached for her hand and worked her fingers out. She paused and let Claire and Ben get a few steps ahead. "Listen, Heather, this is just a Christmas festival, okay? There are lots of people who entered who didn't get anything."

"I know, Mom." She glared at Katie.

"I just don't want you to ruin your whole day over this. You had fun painting it. You didn't have to go outside and do the sports. If you don't get anything, I just…." Katie exhaled, trying to explain hard things to a child was so, so difficult.

"Did you know Theo tried to start two businesses while we were married?" she asked, and that got Heather to actually look at her instead of through her.

"He did?"

"Yes, and they both failed. After the second one went under, we were broke. We had nothing but a bug-infested apartment." Katie didn't want to revisit those memories. "But he kept trying. He told me once that these companies he's doing now were his sixth attempt at a business. Six tries, Heather. Lots of practice. Lots of ideas. Lots of trying and failing and trying again."

"I wish he were here," she said softly. "He's going to like the painting."

"I know, sweetheart." Katie hugged her, hoping her inner fury wasn't showing on the outside. But she was going to kill Theo when she saw him again. For standing her up again. For promising Heather he'd be there and then not coming. Didn't he know what that did to a child?

Of course he didn't. He didn't have children. Theo hadn't had to think about anyone else for a long, long time.

Her phone chimed, and she hastened to pull it out of her purse.

"Is that him?" Heather asked, her voice a bit choked. She wiped her eyes, and Katie wanted it to be Theo so, so badly.

"No, bug. It's Grandma." She turned the phone to Heather so she could read the message. *Good luck with the festival today! Let me know how it goes.*

Katie wanted to cry, then punch something, then cry some more. She held everything so tight as she put her phone back in her purse and took her daughter's hand again. "Come on. Let's go see the painting. Am I going to like it too?"

"Yeah," Heather said. "I hope so."

They moved into the art section, and Katie walked a half-step behind her daughter, every cell in her body on high alert.

"There it is," Heather finally said after they'd rounded three corners and hadn't seen it. The painting hung on the back wall of the community center, and it boasted bright, bold, beautiful Hawaiian colors that showed a beautiful oasis of trees, flowers, shrubs, and....

"Is that our backyard?" Katie asked as she stepped closer. She saw the edge of the deck, and the cat bowls in the back of the patio. "It is. Heather." She exhaled, in total awe of her daughter's talent. "This is incredible."

The painting was probably two feet by two feet, and it made Katie want to find her latest paperback and curl up to read. "I mean, it's so beautiful."

"And a blue ribbon," Claire whispered, and Katie flinched.

"Really? Where?"

"On my name. Mom, look. I got first place."

Joy and relief filled Katie so quickly she almost started crying. Her eyes dropped to the name plate and she saw Heather had named the painting *My Happy Place*.

"Wow, bug. First place on your first painting." She put her arm around her and pulled her into her side. "So, so great, Heather. So great."

They stood there for a few more minutes. Long enough for the pride and euphoria and relief to give way to the absolute anger that Theo had missed this moment with them.

For what? Katie asked herself, and she couldn't let the thought go.

The four of them went for tacos, like they'd planned, and Claire and Ben kept Heather's spirits up throughout the meal. Katie participated when she had to, but both Claire and Ben kept shooting her glances that said they knew she was a ticking time bomb.

"All right," she finally said. "Let's get on home. I'm tired."

She hugged Claire goodbye, and her friend whispered, "Call me as soon as you hear from him."

Katie nodded and she nodded at Ben, who swept his arm around Claire's waist, a worried look on his face. Back at home, Katie changed out of her nice clothes and put on her ratty pajamas. When she went to tuck in Heather, she found her in bed, changed and ready, crying.

"What's wrong, bug?" she asked.

"I don't know," Heather said. "I just...have all these... feelings inside."

So Katie covered her up with her favorite blankets and tucked her stuffed elephant in by her head. Then she climbed into bed with her, and asked, "Good feelings or bad feelings?"

"Both." Heather curled into her, and Katie stroked her hair, her voice automatically starting the nursery rhymes. But she understood Heather's feelings. She had them too. Good ones and bad ones, and she felt like crying too.

But the one person she wanted to be there to hold her while she did was the one person who'd made her feel all the bad feelings.

Where are you, Theo? she thought as her daughter finally quieted enough to fall asleep.

———

An hour later, Katie's phone finally went off, startling her from the movie playing on her laptop. If it was anyone but Theo, she might throw her phone out the window.

But it was Theo, and he said *I'm so so sorry. Something came up, and I rushed back as quickly as I could. I don't suppose you're still at the community center?*

For several long seconds, she considered not answering at all. Did he really think they'd be at the community center almost three hours after he was supposed to meet them? She snorted, her heart hardening against his apology.

No, she typed out, her fingers hovering over the screen, waiting for her to decide if she should send more. In the end, she didn't, just letting that single word zip across the telephone lines to him.

Can I come see you?

It's not me you need to see, she said. She thought of Heather, sobbing in her bed, and she knew some of her feelings were because of Theo not keeping his promise. *But Heather's asleep.*

I'm on my way.

Katie heaved herself out of bed, unsure of what she'd tell Theo when he showed up. All she knew was that she wasn't changing back into regular clothes, and she wasn't going to let her daughter get hurt again.

So when Theo pulled up to the house, she was sitting on the front steps in her purple pajamas, waiting for him. He got out of the car and approached slowly, his head down. At least he looked sorry.

"Hey." He climbed the steps and sat beside her.

"Where were you?" she asked.

"It's a long story."

"I think I deserve to hear it."

He cut a glance at her out of the corner of his eye. "All right. I'm trying to hire more people to take a new client Ben drummed up. There's this ex-FBI agent that lives up on the bluffs, and he was supposed to come down to the office today. Instead, he wouldn't leave the house because he's paranoid, and I ended up at his place." Theo ran both hands through his hair and sighed. "I was there for four hours, and I couldn't find a way out. By the time I got my phone back and could leave, he was convinced I needed to stay the night because there would be snipers on the highway coming back down."

Katie blinked at him. "This isn't a joke to me."

"I'm not joking."

"Heather was *devastated*," she said, her fury rising like the tide. "I realize you don't have children, but you can't make promises to them and then break them. You just can't." She shook her head and looked across the street.

"I'm sorry about that," he said.

"Sometimes sorry isn't enough," she murmured.

"What does that mean?"

"I don't know."

Theo sighed too, but it wasn't the happy kind of sound she wanted to hear from him. "The exhibit will be up tomorrow. I'll take her first thing."

"No," Katie said, shaking her head. "No, we've already gone. She got second place on her sourdough, and she won the children's painting division."

"So I don't get another chance?"

Katie turned toward him. "How many do you think you get?"

"I'm not perfect, Katie."

"I know that." Boy, did she know that. "Neither am I. But you know what? It's not just me anymore, and you weren't there while she cried tonight." Katie drew in a breath. "I think we should take a break."

"No," he said. "I don't want to take a break."

"Yeah, well, I don't want to constantly come second to whatever else happens to come up."

He sucked in a breath, creating a hissing sound, but Katie had finally found the reason the relationship had been bothering her since that missed meeting. "You don't put us first," she said. "And for this to work, we have to come first. I do. Heather does."

"You work too," he said. "You're telling me Heather always comes first for you?"

"Absolutely she does," she said, heat filling her whole body. "The only reason I'm working at all is because my criminal of a husband was dealing drugs. Before moving here, I stayed home full-time with Heather. And when I'm late getting her now, it's also because of someone else. I never *choose* other things over her deliberately." Her chest felt so tight, so tight. "You will always choose your business over us."

"If you really think that, what's been happening all these months?"

"I don't know," she said. "I guess I thought you'd changed. In a lot of ways, you have. But not with work."

"So you've just been waiting for me to screw up, is that it?"

"No," she said.

"I think yes," he said. "Like, you knew this was a problem for you, but instead of talking to me about it, you just led me on, made me think I actually had a chance to get you back, but at the first sign of me doing something you don't like, you're out." He stood up. "You know what, Katie? I'm tired." He went down the steps and on toward his car.

Katie's heart quivered, but she didn't dare call him back. He paused with the door open, one foot in the car. "I'm sorry," he called. "Will that ever be good enough?"

She wanted to reply that of course it was, but she'd already spoken true when she'd said sometimes sorry wasn't enough. Heather needed more than sorry. She deserved more. And Theo worked *a lot*, and Katie didn't think this would be the only time something came up.

"I'm sorry too," she called. "But I don't think this is going to work out."

EIGHTEEN

THEO DROVE AWAY from Katie's house, the absolute worst ending to an awful day. He was utterly exhausted in every way, but he managed to get himself home and up to his condo. He stripped to his boxers and collapsed into bed, but unconsciousness didn't steal him away, give him relief from the agony rippling through his mind.

Things were over with Katie. Again.

How could he have let that happen? Would it have been so hard to reach over Jack and get his phone? Why hadn't he done it? He knew why, but Katie had acted like she didn't even believe the story of him going up the bluff to Jack Harper's house.

"Jack is crackers," he muttered, rolling over to plug in his phone. With that done, and no alarm set for tomorrow, he was finally able to fall asleep.

But he didn't sleep well, always just a breath away from waking up, thinking perhaps Katie had texted him and told him she was wrong, that she did want to keep trying with him, that she loved him.

But when he checked his phone in the morning, she hadn't messaged once. He honestly hadn't expected her to. He dressed and drove down to the community center to see Heather's submissions. He stood in front of her painting for a while, the Saturday crowd ebbing and flowing around him.

Her backyard was his happy place too, and she'd captured the essence of it perfectly. Everything in him mourned the fact that he hadn't been brave enough to snatch his phone and send a text last night. But he'd truly thought Jack Harper would keep him hostage all night if he did.

And he would not be hiring the man, even if he was brilliant. Which meant he needed to find someone else or send The Grocery Guys account to Dallas.

Or give it up completely.

He didn't need more clients. He had plenty of money, and no time. No girlfriend. No happy place in her backyard. He wanted to jump in his car and rush back to her house, beg her to forgive him and give him one more chance.

But he wouldn't. Just like he hadn't followed her when she'd left him twenty years ago, he wasn't going to go beg now either. He left the community center and went to the taco stand, like they'd planned last night.

His phone brightened, and he checked it. His hopes plummeted when he saw Fisher's name on the screen.

Nine-0 Club Christmas party next weekend. Is Katie your plus-one?

Theo felt like throwing up. He'd forgotten about the Nine-0 party, and he hadn't even mentioned it to Katie yet. He actually considered that a win, as she wouldn't have to endure that night alone now.

No, he typed out, feeling like his fingers had entered an alternate dimension where everything happened in slow motion. *I'll be coming with Ben.*

Fisher called, which only annoyed Theo. But he answered with, "Thanks for almost getting me killed."

"Wha—what?"

"Jack Harper is a nutter," Theo said. "He almost wouldn't let me leave his house last night, and he kept me there for hours."

"Really? I mean, I knew he was a little eccentric."

"He's crazy."

"So you're not going to hire him?"

"No," Theo said. "And Katie and I broke up, so I'll just come to the party with Ben, or alone, if that's what you would prefer." Maybe Theo wouldn't go at all, though he had enjoyed last year's shindig quite a lot. It was fun to see the spouses and significant others of the other billionaires, meet their families, watch them interact on a more social level instead of talking business so much.

"You can bring Ben. How close is he to becoming a member?"

"Close, I think," Theo said, though he hadn't checked with Ben on his investments in a while. Ben had hired Lawrence for that, actually.

"If you're not up for coming...." Fisher said.

"I'll be there," Theo said, finding it ironic that it was a promise just like that which had gotten him in trouble in the first place. He sat at a picnic table, surrounded by people, and he felt so very alone. He thought of all the things he wanted to do on this island, and who he wanted to do them with.

The monster zipline still hadn't been conquered, and he still hadn't eaten a burger out at the cattle ranch that Heather had told him about. He'd always wanted more hours in the day, first so he could accomplish more work, and then so he could spend them with Katie.

And now he found himself with several hours in front of him with nothing to do. Well, there was plenty of work to be done on the Gladstone Financial app, or any number of other projects. Problem was, for the first time in years, he didn't want to do the work.

When Katie had left the first time, Theo had fallen into a slump. But he hadn't had a problem getting up and trying something new that day.

"What did you do last time?" he wondered aloud, earning him a glance from a mother sitting with her children nearby. Theo lifted his hand in greeting and got up. He walked down the beachwalk toward his condo, thinking of those days and weeks after Katie had left the first time. He'd thought if he was just successful enough, she would've stayed. If that second business hadn't failed, their marriage wouldn't have suffered the same fate.

But what if that wasn't right?

Katie didn't seem to care about money, something Theo

had a hard time understanding. All he'd ever wanted was to provide a stable life for her and their future family. And that took success and money...didn't it?

Theo arrived at home, his thoughts revolving around Katie and how he could get a third chance with her. With his mind preoccupied, he went over the code Lawrence needed, and he started taking notes on what needed to be changed and added. His mind had always worked well when overburdened, and that was one reason he didn't mind feeling like he had more work to do than hours in the day.

But Katie didn't like that. She didn't want him to work all the time, and Theo paused and blinked, his vision a bit blurry from all the time he spent in front of the computer screen.

"I have to get her back," he said to himself, and Ben answered, "Then go get her back."

He looked over the top of his monitor to see his best friend standing in the doorway. "I tried," he said. "She was so angry."

"You know why, right?"

"I missed the festival."

"No," Ben said, moving forward. "You upset Heather. You broke a promise to a little girl that means the world to Katie. And there's no way she's going to let you hurt her daughter again."

"I can't be perfect," Theo said, desperation coursing through him. "I'm going to make mistakes. I do work a lot." And he didn't want to change all of that. After all, in a perfect world, if he'd had to work last night, he would've made alternate plans with Heather to attend the festival today instead. There would've been compromise. Maybe some disappointment, but definitely compromise.

"You just have to decide what you want, man." Ben exhaled as he sat down.

"I thought I knew that," Theo said, focusing back on the screens in front of him. But the truth was, he wasn't sure of a whole lot anymore. He knew he wanted to keep his promises at work, and in his personal life.

And right now, all he had was his job, so he focused on that, just as he had before. But what if he should be doing something different this time?

———

Christmas music played in the lobby of Sweet Breeze, and Theo basked in the American tradition for several long moments. "Hello, sir," Maxim said, the security guard standing by Fisher's private hallway. "Going up tonight?"

"Yes," he said, and Maxim strode over to the elevator and pushed the button for him. Theo carried several cards in his hand, and he gave one to Maxim.

"Merry Christmas," he said with a smile.

"Thank you, sir." Maxim tucked the card inside his jacket and grinned. "Did you hear that Maine Fitzgerald got engaged?"

"The quarterback?" Theo didn't particularly follow football, but he was a Texan, and the genes were in his blood. "Didn't he get stranded not too long ago?"

"Yeah, with a woman." Maxim's eyebrows went up,

and the elevator doors opened. "I guess they fell madly in love out on that island."

Theo chuckled along with Maxim, who was always good for a piece of island gossip. "Maybe I should try that. I'm going to a party with my business partner. Have you seen Ben yet?"

"No, sir."

Theo nodded, said, "Merry Christmas," one more time, and got on the elevator alone. He rested his head against the cool metal as the car shot up, wondering if he could survive another twenty years of life by himself.

The weight of the whole hotel seemed to press down on him, and he honestly didn't think he could. On Fisher's floor, the holiday music intensified in volume, as did the general excitement in the air.

He entered the penthouse to laughter, and merriment, and glowing Christmas tree lights. Gifts sprouted out from under the tree, and Theo grinned at the evergreen before focusing on his friends. They all wore their formal clothes, as he expected, and stood in groups, chatting. Some had glasses of sparkling sodas, and some sipped water, and others nursed flavored colas—like Lawrence.

Theo felt out of place there, without anyone on his arm, and he wondered what Katie would've thought of an upscale party like this. A bolt of sadness struck him, and that seemed to draw every eye to him.

Stacey bent her head together with Esther and Tawny, and then all three of them left their husbands and came toward him.

"Oh, boy," he said, raising his hands in surrender. "What did I do?"

"Where's Katie?" Stacey asked.

"Probably at home," he said. "Look, you guys already know we broke up."

"But you loved her," Stacey said, a whine in her voice.

"I mean...." Theo looked away. "When your husbands mess up, what does it take to make things right with you?" He looked at the three women, deciding they were a decent sample group.

"Jewelry," Tawny said, and Sasha, Jasper's wife, joined them.

"Oh, I love jewelry," she said. "Who are we buying for?" She glanced at Theo and gasped. "Katie? Are you asking Katie to marry you?"

"She just got back from Switzerland," Tawny said.

"I like a romantic date," Esther said. "Just us. No kids. No talk about pineapples or profits or anything like that."

"She won't go out with me," Theo said as gently as he could.

"But when she does," Esther said. "Make sure it's romantic. No kids. No talk about work or websites or anything like that." She gave him a very pointed look that stabbed him right to the heart.

"I try not to," he said.

"Yeah, I know," Esther said. "You men and your businesses." She lifted her drink to her lips. "Some of us don't care."

"You own a business too," he pointed out.

"Yeah, but only in paper. I don't drive anymore, and I hired a full-time manager. So it's not the same as it was."

Theo wanted that for Katie, and an idea started to take shape in his mind. He imagined a life for her where she still owned Clean Sweep, but only on paper. She didn't have to scrub any floors and she could have a full-time manager take care of everything. Someone she trusted... someone like Claire.

"He's got a look in his eye," Stacey said, drawing his attention back to her.

"Do you like being home with the kids?" he asked them.

"Yeah," Esther said. "It's a different kind of work, but I like it."

"I think Katie liked it too."

"Oh, and you think you can get her to fall madly in love with you, hire a manager, and stay home with Heather?" Stacey looked like she'd swallowed a mouthful of lemon juice.

"Bad idea?" he asked.

"She should be involved in that decision," Tawny said. "I don't have children yet, but when I do, I'd want to be able to talk with Tyler about what we'll do."

"Your husband doesn't work," Esther pointed out, and Tawny looked at her.

"So? You think that means he wants to be Mister Mom?" She folded her arms.

"Maybe," Esther said. "He'd be good at it."

"And I wouldn't?"

"That's not what I'm saying." Esther looked at Stacey. "Help me out."

"Do you want to quit the beach yoga?" Stacey asked, and Theo felt like an outsider in the conversation.

"No," Tawny said. "It's only part-time anyway, and Tyler's already said he'd love to have the baby while I'm gone."

A hush fell over the women, and then Stacey squealed, almost deafening Theo. He flinched away from the sound as the four women in front of him started jumping up and down and laughing.

"What's going on?" Lawrence asked as he joined Theo.

"What did you do?" Jasper asked, also coming over.

"I have no idea," Theo said.

All the women were talking at once, and Theo couldn't find one of their voices and follow the thread. Tyler arrived on-scene, and he said, "She told the girls, then?"

"Told them what?" Jasper yelled over the uproar. Theo glanced around and found everyone at the party watching.

Tyler stepped over to Tawny, who was crying, and touched her back. She turned toward him, and the posse broke up. "So, Tawny and I are expecting," he called out above the Christmas tunes. Tawny wiped her eyes and grinned, and Tyler looked pretty pleased himself.

Theo's mouth filled with bitterness. Unless he married someone much younger than him, he'd never be a father. It was something he hadn't thought he wanted—until he was standing there watching the joy on his friend's faces.

Until he thought about Heather, and how much he'd

enjoyed talking to her, and swimming with her, and watching her cook.

He turned to leave, to go to Katie and convince her that he wouldn't choose work above her. Because without her, his success meant nothing. Without her, his money was meaningless. His entire life was meaningless.

"Hey," Ben said, blocking his escape. "What's going on?"

Theo watched all the hand-shaking, congratulating, and hugging, feeling nothing but hollow inside. "Tawny's pregnant," he said.

"Oh, that's great," Ben said, and of course it was great. Christmas was great. The food was great, and the people he was with were great. Exchanging presents and laughing was great.

But Theo didn't really feel like he was a part of the greatness. He felt like it was happening around him, passing him by, like so many years of his life already had.

And he wanted to taste the greatness. Experience it. Breathe it in and live it.

To do that, he needed Katie and Heather in his life. He needed to start spending some of his money instead of working, working, working to make more of it.

Tomorrow, he told himself. Tomorrow, he'd figure out how to get Katie back into his life and how to start truly living it.

NINETEEN

KATIE STARED at Heather as she angrily slapped cheese slices on buttered bread. "You can't talk to me like that."

"Why not, Mom?"

"Because I'm your mother, and I deserve more respect than that." Her own anger rose, but she worked to tamp it down. The past couple of weeks had been difficult to say the least, with Heather upset that Katie had broken up with Theo, and then with learning that now that her painting was finished, she'd have to go back outside and do the sports in her after-care club.

She'd already tried to fake a cold, a sprained ankle, and a fake disease where she couldn't be in the sun. And now she'd just told Katie that her life would be better if they'd stayed in Kansas, because at least then she'd get to see her dad on holidays.

Her Christmas card from her father had not arrived yet,

and with only two days until Christmas, time was running out.

"You don't need to make me a sandwich," Katie said as she turned away from her daughter's upset face. "I'm not that hungry." She walked out of the kitchen, unable to deal with Heather's outburst right now.

Katie had been having a hard enough time unknotting her own emotions and managing her own grief over the loss of Theo for the second time in her life. But this time, it was doubly hard, because she had Heather to deal with too. She'd had a crying fit about every other night for the past two weeks, and now she'd just turned mean.

Katie had looked up some information on preteens, and Heather was showing all the signs of a normal, regular, almost-teenager, but Katie didn't have to like it. Or be insulted by her child, a person who didn't have the experience or wisdom to make life decisions.

She closed her bedroom door behind her and pressed her back into it, breathing in deep through her nose. "Okay," she said as she exhaled. Her phone had been dreadfully silent lately, with only her maids texting or calling about work. She hadn't dared change her relationship status on GBS, though she felt lost and in need of some direction in her love life.

Retreating to the recliner beside the window, she sat and looked outside. She'd taken up this position a lot over the past couple of weeks since Theo had gotten in his car, asking her if his apology would ever be enough.

She'd gone through a range of emotions, from guilt over not giving him the benefit of the doubt, to denial that she'd been waiting for him to screw up so she could dump him. She didn't want that.

Did she?

Katie had gone around and around, through, over, under, and back around her actions and feelings and thoughts. She'd admitted that maybe she'd been selfish, and she knew better than most that a real relationship required sacrifice and selflessness. Maybe she'd over-reacted to the situation with Heather, as she was also mad at Katie for removing Theo from their lives.

"I was trying to protect her," she whispered to the glass, but she knew she'd been trying to protect herself. And she'd failed.

The doorbell rang, and Katie twisted in her chair, trying to think if she was expecting someone. She wasn't, not even Claire. Maybe it was one of the neighbors, with another bag of white chocolate popcorn or a plate of cookies. Katie always hated taking the gifts, because she never reciprocated.

When the house stayed silent, she stayed in her chair. Heather knew better than to answer the door without her, so it was especially upsetting to hear voices in the hallway. She sprang to her feet, her heart racing but her body staying stubbornly where it was.

Someone knocked, and then Heather said, "Mom?" through a crack in the door.

Katie tiptoed across the room and asked, "Who is it? Why did you answer the door?"

Heather ducked into the room, an unreadable expression on her face. "You left your phone in the kitchen," she hissed. "And I saw the texts, so I knew who it was."

"Well, who is it?"

"Theo." Heather grinned like she'd just gotten her entire wish list from Santa Claus himself. "Mom, it's *Theo*."

"What in the world?" Katie fluffed her hair, dropping her hand when she realized what she was doing. "I don't want to see him."

"Come on, Mom. He says he just wants to talk to us."

"Us?"

"Yeah, both of us, together." Heather's hope faded, getting replaced with the sour look that Katie was becoming used to. "I tried to get him to come eat with me, but he insisted he talk to us both."

Katie turned away from Heather. "I know you like him, bug. But I honestly don't think it's going to work between us, no matter what he says."

"But *why*, Mom?"

"If you think I work a lot, you have no idea." Katie faced her daughter and lifted her chin. "You know how he only comes over on Sundays? That's because he works at all hours every other day of the week. Is that what you want?" She edged forward, feeling a spark in her that had been absent since the break-up. "You already have a dad who's not around. You want another one?"

Heather looked like she'd been slapped, and Katie regretted the strength in her words. "I'm sorry, bug," she said, deflating as quickly as she'd gotten fired up. "But that's the truth, and I'm trying to protect you from another situation like the Christmas festival." She gathered her daughter into a hug, surprised when Heather let her.

Her arms were surprisingly strong for a girl who didn't like PE or any kind of sports. Then she stepped back and said, "Well, I'm going to talk to him." She moved around Katie and opened the door before Katie could do anything.

"She doesn't want to see you," Heather said, truthfully, and the statement made Katie cringe. The door closed just as she lunged for it. Her knuckles hit the wood and she flinched away before scrambling to twist the knob.

"Heather," she said, and both Heather and Theo turned to face her.

Katie's heart boomed in her chest with loud beats. The sight of Theo's handsome face, the anxiety in his expression, the way he watched her with those intoxicating eyes.

"I just want to talk for a few minutes," he finally said, breaking the tense silence between them. "Maybe on the back deck?" He put his arm around Heather and said, "As I was saying, I saw your painting and it was beautiful. So great." They moved down the hall together, and Katie hated seeing them walk away from her.

So she got herself moving after them. She felt like a newborn, like she'd never taken two steps together before. But she did get down the hallway and through the kitchen and onto the back deck with her daughter and the man she suspected she couldn't truly live without.

"I just want to say I'm sorry for missing it a couple of weeks ago," he said. "Sometimes things happen that keep me from doing what I really want to do." His gaze flickered to Katie's, but then he focused back on Heather. "Sometimes that happens, you know?"

"I know," she said. "My teacher said once that we could have a movie on Friday, but then there was a fire drill and we didn't have time."

Theo smiled, and it was filled with soft love. "Yeah, kind of like that." He sobered and folded his arms. "I was wondering if you wanted to go to breakfast with me tomorrow. Then we can go shopping."

Heather looked at Katie, but Theo said, "Oh, just you and me, Heather. Your mom's actually not invited."

"Not invited?" Katie's voice pitched up. "It's Christmas Eve."

"I'll have her back by noon," Theo said coolly, his expression turning a smidge harder when he looked fully at her. "I just want to spend some time with her alone." He took a step toward Katie and then fell back to his position by the swing again. "You too, if you'd like. Maybe we could go to dinner tomorrow night."

Katie wanted to blurt yes, she'd love to, but she still wasn't sure which angle Theo was playing.

"Can I, Mom?" Heather asked, and Katie found she couldn't deny her.

"Sure, sweetheart."

"Great," Theo said. "I'll pick you up about eight, okay?"

Heather beamed at him, then Katie, and she said, "Okay. I'm going to go check on the cats." And she skipped off, leaving Katie to face Theo alone.

"What are you doing?" she asked, narrowing her eyes at him.

"Apologizing," he said. "To her. To you." He did take that step toward her this time, his gaze tracking Heather for a few seconds. "I want to take her Christmas shopping."

"Claire—"

"I know," he said, lifting his hand as if to quiet her. "I've already spoken to Claire. She told me she takes Heather Christmas shopping on Christmas Eve, and I begged her to let me do it this year."

He took another step toward her, and Katie could practically feel the warmth from his hand as it curved down the side of her face, though he was still a few strides away from her. "I want to take you out. Just the two of us. No kids. No talk about business. Just something romantic, so you'll know I'm dying without you." He stepped again. "A slow, painful death that seems to go on and on no matter what I do."

One more step. "And I can't keep doing it. I love you. I want you back in my life. I've hired more people, so I'll have more time. I mean, I can't control certain things, like if someone files a complaint about my app that needs immediate attention. But I don't have to build every website and every app."

He took another step and now he stood right in front of her. His voice had muted at some point after he'd said the words, "I love you."

Those three words echoed endlessly in her head, and she startled when he put his hand in hers and then slid his fingers up her arm. "So what do you think?" he asked. "Dinner tomorrow? We can start again?"

Katie's eyes drifted closed as his hand moved into her hair. "I don't know."

"What else can I say? What can I do?"

Katie looked up at him, everything inside her softening. The seconds stretched, and the forgiveness she needed surged through her. "I love you too."

He blinked, obviously surprised.

"Is this crazy?" she asked, genuinely wanting to know.

"No," he whispered, gathering her fully into his arms now. And it was the only place she wanted to be. The comfort and relief she felt made tears come to her eyes, and she wrapped her arms around his back to hold him tight.

He stepped back only a moment later, his eyes once again cutting to the back of the yard where Heather fed the cats. "So I'll see you tomorrow then."

Katie pressed her lips together and nodded. Theo nodded too, called, "'Bye, Heather," and reached for the doorknob.

He stepped through before Katie realized he was going to leave without kissing her. And that simply wouldn't do. So she followed him into the house, cast a quick look at Heather, still busy with the cats, and went with him all the way to the front porch.

"Theo," she said, and he turned back to her. She wasn't sure what to say. She'd said she loved him. He'd said it too, but it wasn't in the same conversation. So she just reached up and cradled his face in her hands and tipped up on her toes, bringing her mouth to his.

She kept contact for only a moment, then she said, "I love you. You can't leave without a kiss," and she met his mouth again. This time, she kissed him like she loved him, and he kissed her back the same way.

TWENTY

THEO COULDN'T BELIEVE Katie was kissing him. If he'd known all he needed to do was show up at her house and tell her he was dying without her, he'd have done it weeks ago. Instead, he'd been sleeping poorly and making plans since the Nine-0 Club holiday party for the most romantic dinner he could put together on short notice, on Christmas Eve.

And he was still going to do that. Oh, yes, he was. He didn't think all could be resolved in a few minutes of conversation, but he wanted to keep kissing Katie, and keep coming to spend time with her in her back yard and keep her in his life permanently this time.

"I love you too," he whispered, kissing her one final time. "I'm so sorry."

She leaned her forehead against his, her breathing quite uneven. "I know, Theo. You can tell me all about it tomorrow at dinner." She stepped back, removing her touch from his face, opened the door, and went inside before he could say or do anything else.

He stood on her steps, stunned and still a bit drunk from her kiss. "Tomorrow at dinner," he said to her front door. When he arrived back at the office, voices came from the other room, where he and Ben and hired two more people to work out of the Getaway Bay branch, and he'd authorized the hiring of twenty-five more developers and coders in the Dallas office. Half of them were set to start the second day after Christmas, and Theo paused in the doorway of the second office, nothing stealing his attention or time at the moment.

"Getting settled in?" he asked.

Tyson Longmore turned and grinned. "Almost ready. Ben's getting us hooked up to the WiFi."

"Theo," Ben said without looking up from the screen. This room now had three desks, with twice that many monitors. Ben had moved into Theo's office, which was where he worked ninety percent of the time anyway. "How'd it go this morning?"

"Good," he said. "All set for tomorrow."

That got Ben to stand up. His eyes met Theo's, and a slow smile spread his lips. "Really? All set?"

"All set," he said. "So your guy better have the beach set up."

Ben grabbed his phone off the desk and started texting. Several seconds later, he said, "He's ready." He grinned fully now. "You guys back together?"

Theo thought of the kiss on Katie's front porch. "Sort

of," he said, his stomach turning warm. "I'm still going to need to pull out all the stops though."

So he'd take Heather shopping and they'd find something wonderful for her mother. And then he'd see if he and Katie could take "I love you" all the way down the aisle to another "I do."

The following morning, he waited in front of Katie's house a few minutes before eight, glad he was early and not rushing. It was a nice feeling. A good feeling.

Heather opened the door a minute later and came bounding down the steps, her dark hair curled and bouncing with the movement. "Heya," she said as she opened the door and got in the car beside him.

"Hi, Heather. You hungry?" He caught sight of Katie leaning in the doorway, and his heart skipped several times. He wanted to jump out of the car, dash up the steps, and kiss her until he couldn't see straight.

Instead, he waved at her and backed out of the driveway, saying, "Where's the best place on the island for breakfast?"

"I don't know. We never go out to eat." Heather looked at him. "I was thinking my mom would like one of those necklaces from Lightning Point. You know, the ones you were telling us about with the pieces of petrified lightning on them?"

"You think so?" Theo asked, trying to chat and think and navigate all at the same time. But it wasn't like he got out to breakfast a lot either. In fact, Ben usually brought back doughnuts.

Doughnuts.

He picked up his phone and put in Nuts About Dough so his app would take him there. Once it started talking to him, he asked, "What other ideas do you have? We could go to the mall."

"Claire usually takes me to the drug store and I get my mom candy or something."

"Well, we can do that, too," Theo said. "But I think we can get more than candy."

Heather let a few seconds go by. "Because you're rich, right?"

Theo chuckled and turned out of the neighborhood where Katie lived. "Yeah, I have a little bit of money."

Heather started talking about the painting and the festival, as well as another project she'd started to work on. Theo bought her as many doughnuts as she wanted, and they ate them in the shop, at a tiny table that he could barely fit his legs underneath. A steady stream of people went in and out of the shop, and only a few of them stayed.

After that, Theo took Heather to the drug store for the candy she wanted, and then they started the journey around the island to Lightning Point. Theo thought they might not be open, and he made a quick phone call to the visitor's center to find out.

"They're open," he said to Heather. "So we're in luck." They arrived several minutes later, and Heather went straight to the jewelry cases and started looking. Someone came to help them, and Heather had the woman get out several pieces, finally deciding on one that looked like a warped tree root and had a faint blue tint.

"She'll like this one," Heather said, obvious pride in her voice. Theo grinned at her, paid for the necklace, and said he'd wrap it and have it ready when he came to pick up Katie that night.

They walked back to the car, and Heather had her seatbelt buckled before she asked, "So are you going to marry my mom?"

"Oh, um." Theo buckled his own belt. "I don't know, sweetheart."

"But you love her, right?"

"I do," Theo said.

"But you work too much," she said.

"I'm working less now," he said. "At least that's the goal."

"I never see my dad," she said. "And I don't want another dad I never see."

Theo's fingers tightened on the steering wheel, but he had no idea what to say. None at all.

"He hasn't even sent a card this year," she said, her voice squeaking. "And he always sends a card." She swiped at her eyes, and Theo wanted to fix everything in her life for her so she never had to watch the mail and hope it had a card in it.

"Maybe it's just late," he said, his own voice a little froggy.

Heather didn't say anything, and they pulled into her driveway a few minutes later.

"I'll see you tonight," Theo said. "I'll slip you the necklace and you can put it under the tree, okay?"

"Okay." Heather turned and looked at him. "Thanks, Theo."

"Yeah." He got out of the car and walked with her up the steps. He gave her a big hug and said, "I'm sure you'll get a card from your dad, okay?"

"You think so?"

"I hope so." Theo beamed down at her. "And hey, I'll bring you a card if it'll make you feel better." He knew it wouldn't, but she nodded and went inside the house.

He stayed on the porch for a moment, almost desperate to make a Christmas card show up at this house from a penitentiary in Kansas and utterly powerless to make that happen.

———

Hours later, he stood on the same porch, this time dressed in his finest suit, his shiniest shoes, and having just gotten a haircut from the woman in his building who had five kids in a two-bedroom condo. He'd given her a large tip and wished her a Merry Christmas before putting every piece of himself in place, checking with Ben to make sure dinner would go without a hitch, and driving over here.

He knocked and waited, his nerves almost shot and the date hadn't even started yet.

Katie opened the door, and she wore a pink dress that was a couple of shades above white. Her hair was all piled up on top of her head, and she wore just the right amount of makeup to enhance her natural beauty.

Theo's cells vibrated and he whistled at her. "Wow,

you've always taken my breath away." He swept his arm around her waist slowly, giving her the opportunity to step back, stay out of reach, if she wanted.

"I love you," he whispered. He wasn't going to say it again so soon, but he simply couldn't restrain himself. Before she could respond, he drew in a sharp breath and said, "Let's go to dinner."

He stepped back, taking her hand in his, and leading her down the steps. He played every move perfectly, paying attention to her and opening the door for her, asking her if she was comfortable, and then setting the sports car toward the beach.

"Where are we going?" she asked.

"I've arranged something," he said evasively, easing into a parking lot and searching for the building he wanted. He finally spotted it and parked as close as he could.

"There aren't any restaurants down here," she said as he unbuckled his seatbelt. She didn't move a muscle, and Theo had seen that stubborn look on her face before.

"We're eating on the beach," he said. "A private affair, catered by this social hall." He nodded toward it. "Now come on. Your chicken is probably getting cold as we speak." He chuckled, and he was glad when she joined him at the front of the car.

They walked up the sidewalk and into the hall, where a man in a tuxedo met them with a smile and kind words. He led them to the table-for-two on the beach, which had candles and roses and billowy streamers on the back of the chairs.

"Theo," Katie said as they approached. "This is beautiful." The sun was almost down, but the remaining light set the perfect scene for romance.

He waited until the other man left, and then he said, "I really do want to make things work between us."

"Theo, I know you do."

"And?" he asked, meeting her eye. "Do I have a chance?"

She titled her head and looked at him, and then a team of people descended on them, bringing bread and butter, crab bisque, and a green salad. A flurry of activity happened as plates and bowls got set and adjusted, and then everyone melted away as quickly as they had come.

"So I know I said we wouldn't talk business," Theo said as he spread his napkin across his lap. "I came to my money late in life. More belatedly than I would've wanted or that I'd planned for. But I don't care about any of it. Not without you. My bank account doesn't make me smile. Doesn't keep me warm at night." He took a deep breath. "That's what I want from you. I want to smile when I wake up next to you, and I want to make you laugh, and I want to spend the rest of my life with you, whether I have a job or money, or whether I don't."

He looked at her, raw and vulnerable, wishing she'd say something. When she didn't, he said, "So maybe we simply got together too early in life. Maybe it's our time to be together, even if it is a little belatedly."

She lifted a spoonful of bisque to her lips and sipped. "Mm." She nodded and swallowed. "Maybe you're right." She ducked her head, and when she looked up at him through her eyelashes. "I think you definitely have a chance."

Theo grinned and picked up his glass of water. "Great. To us." He clinked his glass against hers, more love flowing through him than he knew how to feel.

The conversation turned light after that, and they talked about everything and nothing. They ate through the main course and the cheesecake dessert before another lull fell over them.

"So," Theo said, reaching into his pocket and feeling the ring there. He picked up a long-stemmed rose with his free hand and stood. He went around the table and knelt down in the sand. "I love you, and I know I've heard you say you love me as recently as yesterday." He produced the ring and held it next to the rose. "I want you in my life forever, even if we're getting started a little later than most people. I want to be a family with you and Heather. Will you marry me?"

Katie stared at the rose, then the diamond, at least thirty seconds passing. Each one felt like torture to Theo, but he *knew* Katie. She needed time to process, and he was determined to give her that time.

"I do love you," she said, finally lifting her eyes to his. Theo saw hope and desire swimming there, along with the softer emotions of love and adoration. "And of course I'll marry you."

A smile burst onto Theo's face, and he slipped the ring onto Katie's finger before kissing her. "Best Christmas ever," he whispered against her lips and both of them chuckled. Then he kissed his fiancée again, pure joy radiating through him that he could have the happy ending with her that he'd always imagined.

"Okay," she said, still holding his face close to hers. "But this time, I want an amazing honeymoon to anywhere in the world I want. And then we can take one with Heather." She giggled, and Theo touched his nose to hers. "Okay?"

"Whatever you want, love," he said. "Whatever you want."

———

Read on for a sneak peek of the first chapter of **THE ISLAND HOUSE, Book 1 in the Getaway Bay Romance series,** right here in Getaway Bay! The world just keeps expanding, and you'll get to meet Charlotte and the man she finds living in her house…

SNEAK PEEK! THE ISLAND HOUSE CHAPTER ONE

CHARLOTTE MADSEN DISEMBARKED from the plane, taking a deep breath of the Hawaii air. Though she'd come from an island, this one felt completely different—exactly what she needed. She went down the skybridge, glad she didn't have to walk straight into the airport. She wanted a view of this new place she was determined to make her new home.

An image of the beach house she'd bought, with its crumbling walls and broken windows, crept into her mind. The jungle had also tried to reclaim the house, one vine and one brick at a time.

She'd gotten the house for dirt cheap, which suited her needs as she started this new chapter of her life.

Not a new chapter, she told herself. A completely new volume needed to begin now that her husband—oops, ex-husband—had married his girlfriend only ten days after the divorce was final.

And Charlotte?

On the eleventh day after the divorce from her husband of eleven years, she'd bought a practically demolished beach house over five thousands miles from where she lived.

And now she was here, in Getaway Bay, to well, get away from everything and everyone she'd known in the last thirty-seven years.

She took a deep breath, her to-do list growing exponentially in her mind. First, luggage. She'd brought as much as she thought she'd need to get through the first two weeks. After that, she hoped to have a job and a way to buy whatever she hadn't brought with her.

Thankfully, the beach house came "furnished," which the seller had confirmed included a bed, a dining set, all appliances, and a sectional couch. So she'd at least have somewhere to sleep, eat, and watch TV on her first night on the island.

Not that Charlotte watched a lot of TV. In fact, she couldn't stand sitting still, and the last seven hours she'd spent on the plane was enough to drive her to madness.

She tipped a man with a huge luggage cart, and he helped her heave her standard, black suitcases off the belt. She stood with them in the taxi line, the heat and humidity still pretty high though it was officially fall on the island. Perhaps Hawaii didn't care what the calendar said.

When it was finally her turn, the cab driver helped her get all her bags in the trunk, and she sank into the back seat with a sigh. The corners of her lips pulled up, and she barely remembered what it felt like to smile.

But she'd done it. Despite what her mother had said. In spite of what her friends had counseled her to do. Charlotte had indeed sold the house she'd lived in for over a decade, nearly everything else she owned, and moved almost five thousand miles, literally from one side of the country to the other.

So while her heart had been through a shredder and then grilled into a lump of coal, she'd survived. The last four months had been one upheaval after another, starting with the words, "I want a divorce. I've met someone else."

She wasn't quite sure where the journey would end, but she rather liked the way she'd been welcomed to the island with "Aloha," a smile, and a flower lei. She breathed in the heady perfume from the flowers and watched the brilliant blue water go by as the driver took her to her new home.

"This is where you're living?" he asked as he pulled off the main highway and onto a dirt road.

"Is this Cinder Road?" Charlotte peered through the window, but she had no idea what she was looking for.

"Yes," he said.

"Then this is it. I was told the house was at the end of the road, overlooking the bays." Both bays, which apparently there were two in Getaway Bay. The main bay which was named after the island, and the east bay, which was starting to become as popular and well-developed as the one to the west.

The owner of the house had tried to get more for the views, but Charlotte's real estate agent had talked him down. It hadn't been that hard, because the property had been on the market for seven months, and Charlotte supposed she had one thing to be thankful for: She had gotten this place and the surrounding land for a killer deal.

The cab rumbled along, but the road seemed to go forever, finally turning a bit to reveal the two-story house Charlotte had seen online. "There it is."

"Are you sure?" The driver leaned forward with both hands on the wheel, his voice absolutely dubious.

"Yes," she said. "As close as you can get, please." She pulled out her wallet and leafed through her remaining cash. Several twenties, a few tens, and a dozen hundreds she had concealed in the zippered pocket of her purse.

She had enough to tip this guy to help her get her bags at least inside the front door. Then...well, then Charlotte wasn't entirely sure what she'd do. She had no car and no groceries. Would a pizza company deliver here? Could they even find it? While it was centrally located overlooking both bays, it wasn't exactly in a populated area.

The cab eased to a stop behind an SUV, which set Charlotte's heart to racing. "That's odd," she said. Maybe her real estate agent had decided to meet her. Amy had asked for her flight information, but Charlotte hadn't heard anything else from her.

"What's odd?" the driver asked. He turned to look at her with concern in his eyes. "Are you sure you want me to leave you here alone?"

Charlotte wasn't sure of much anymore, but she nodded anyway. "If you could help me with the bags, I'd be grateful." She held out a twenty-dollar bill between her fingers, and the driver got out of the car.

Taking another look at the huge, hulking black SUV, she determined that Amy would never drive such a thing. No, they hadn't met in person, but Amy was an overly tan woman in her late forties, and Charlotte imagined her to drive a sporty, red convertible, not this three-ton monstrosity.

She got out of the cab and stretched her sore back. She'd skipped her beach yoga classes for the past four months, as they were simply too hard to attend with all of her friends. They flashed sad faces at her, asked about her ex and what she was going to do now, and Charlotte simply couldn't handle it.

The amount of work this house required extended to the exterior, and Charlotte hoped she had enough knowledge and strength to get it all done. She'd done plenty of renovations on the interior of buildings, everything from the community center gym to individual rooms at one of the swankiest hotels off the coast of South Carolina, where she'd come from.

She also had experience in designing and re-doing landscapes, so she wasn't worried about the weeds and wild grasses waving in the breeze coming off the bays. But she didn't have much experience with roofs, or exterior stone, or gutters.

The driver stepped past the big SUV and deposited the first round of bags, returning for a second before Charlotte got herself in gear. She took out the key that had shown up in her mailbox two weeks ago and fitted it into the lock. With the door open, she heaved in the two bags the driver had brought up, and directed him to place the next two beside them.

When she had all her earthly belongings inside the house, she smiled, ran her hands through her shoulder-length hair, and thanked the driver.

He gave her one more look before pocketing his tip and heading back to his cab. She waited until the rumble of his motor couldn't be heard any longer, and then she closed the door, sealing herself inside the house she'd bought sight-unseen.

"Okay." She pushed her breath out and turned to face the rest of the house.

She'd taken one step when something clanged from further inside. "Hello?" she said, nowhere near loud enough for anyone to hear. Heck, she could barely hear herself.

Something hissed, and then the very human sound of a grunt followed. Charlotte's heart ricocheted around inside her chest. There was someone inside her house.

She entered the kitchen and stepped around the bar to find a pair of masculine legs and a torso sticking out from underneath the sink. He wore jeans and work boots, and maybe the owner had hired a plumber to help get her off on the right foot.

"Come on," he grumbled, clearly straining against something under the sink.

"Hello?" she said again—loud enough this time—at the same time whatever he was twisting gave against his strength. He yelped as water started spraying out from underneath the sink—and from the faucet.

The cold spray hit Charlotte in the face, and she cried

out too, lifting her hands to shield her eyes in a natural reaction. She backed up, sputtering, as the man unfolded himself from beneath the sink and stood up.

"You didn't turn off the water main?" she asked.

He glared at her, water dripping from the ends of his dark hair, his nose, and his chin. "Obviously."

"Why not?"

"I didn't know where it was."

Water continued to spray everywhere, and while Charlotte had been planning to replace the cabinets, she didn't think she'd have to do it the very night she arrived.

"Do you know where it is?" he asked, a measure of hope in his voice.

"I just got here," she said. "Of course I don't know where the water main is."

"Well, we have to do something." His light blue T-shirt was soaking wet, sticking to impressive muscles in his arms and chest. Whoever this plumber was, Charlotte hoped she would have another need to call him.

He crawled back under the sink and started clanging around. The spray lessened by about half, and he groaned again, finally man-handling whatever connection was leaking into submission.

Charlotte wiped her face, her fingers coming away smeared with black. Her past self would've been mortified to be seen like this, but her Getaway Bay self didn't care. She'd expected problems at her new house. She just hadn't planned on them being two-hundred-twenty pounds of man-flesh. Dripping wet man-flesh.

She swallowed as the plumber got to his feet again.

"Who are you?" she asked. Maybe she didn't want to hire him again. A plumber who didn't turn off the water before he started working didn't seem all that professional.

"Dawson Dane," he said, extending his soaking wet hand for her to shake. He wore a couple of days worth of hair on his face, and it had come in dark with flecks of gray, just like the hair on his head.

Oh, my. He was extremely good-looking, and his deep, brown eyes glinted with one of those Aloha greetings. "And you?"

"Charlotte Madsen," she said, almost tripping over her new last name. Well, it was her old last name, but she hadn't used it for a while, and she was still getting used to introducing herself with her maiden name.

She shook his hand, one more question to ask him. "What are you doing in my house, Dawson?"

He blinked, not bothering to wipe any water from his eyelashes. "I live here."

———

THE ISLAND HOUSE, Book 1 in the Getaway Bay Romance series is now available.

Read on for a sneak peek of THE PERFECT STORM, Book 1 in the Stranded in Getaway Bay Romances series!

SNEAK PEEK! THE PERFECT STORM CHAPTER ONE

EDEN MCLAUGHLIN TUCKED her blonde hair behind her ear, the Hawaiian spring wind trying to whip it right off her head. Once she got around the corner up ahead, she'd get some relief.

If only she could get the same reprieve from her thoughts simply by rounding a corner. But no, they continued to go round and round even after she got away from the wind. Deciding to take a break, she found a level piece of ground on the trail she'd escaped to in the wilds of Hawaii—if such a thing could be found.

And it could. Getaway Bay was thriving and growing, but there were still plenty of off-the-beaten-path trails and hikes and opportunities on the island. Sure, she had to drive a little. Yes, hers was the only car in the parking lot— which was little more than a patch of dirt next to a non-marked trailhead.

But this kind of back-country exploring was what Eden

thrived on. She sat down and pulled out the survival tool she'd jimmy-rigged to be everything she needed while hiking. Part knife, part can opener, part pair of scissors, it literally had everything—even a compartment for a solar blanket and a six-foot length of cord she could use for a dozen purposes.

And no one wanted it.

"Billionaires." She scoffed out the word as she pulled the portable stove from her pack. Another invention of hers, she could heat a single serving of whatever she wanted in something the size of a can of beans.

None of the billionaire investors that had flocked to Fisher DuPont's huge eyesore of a hotel on the beach wanted to give her any money to get her line of survival gear off the ground. Her latest meeting had been yesterday with a man named Darius Blood. Yes, Blood.

"More like blood*sucker*," Eden muttered as she got the container of chicken casserole from her pack and scooped it into the can. It had two bottoms, one of which was connected to the other with thin strips of metal, allowing her to stuff grass and small sticks into the gap between the two.

Using her multipurpose tool, which also held matches, she lit the debris and got the flame going. No need to just pack sandwiches anymore. The speeches she'd prepared for her products lingered in her mind, always just out of reach. Ready to be called upon, should she get asked a question in line at the grocery store or on an elevator.

After all, she understood the seven degrees of separation better than almost anyone, and it could be that the cashier could have a brother who knew someone, who knew who owned the biggest and most profitable survival company in Getaway Bay.

Explore Getaway Bay.

Eden had tried to find out who really owned the company. It seemed like every door that opened, five more closed—and she worked as a tour guide for the outdoor department of the company. And she still had no idea who really signed her checks.

Not that there were literally any checks to sign. Not in this digital age.

Sometimes Eden wanted to rewind time, go back to when she had to have cash to buy something, and every-thing passed from person to person. Now, people could buy whole islands with virtual money, and Eden didn't understand any of it. She loved the land, the island, the act of going outside and exploring.

And that was what she did, six days a week. Well, seven if her own exploration of Getaway Bay on her day off counted.

The ocean in front of her brought a small measure of comfort, and she watched the horizon, wondering how long it took for the water way out there to crash against the rocks on the cliffs below her.

Probably as long as it had taken Jeremy to know he didn't want to see her again. She'd been on six first dates in the past couple of months, and she couldn't get a man to commit to a second.

Maybe she talked too much about her inventions. Maybe she didn't talk enough. She'd tried both and failed both times. She told herself it didn't matter, because between working in the shed in her backyard to make awesome outdoor products, her real day job, and all her investment meetings, she certainly didn't have time for a boyfriend.

She'd tried the app that had sent the island into a tailspin—Getaway Bay Singles—but she'd struck out there too.

Eden leaned her head back against the rocks, deciding this week just sucked and she needed to hang in there until next week.

Next week, she'd be on the submarine, her favorite tour, and that would make this week better. She had no more investment meetings, and she'd just take a break from the shed.

That all decided, she ate her chicken and rice, her mood lifted somewhat by the food and the plan to move forward. Still with her back against the cliff, she pulled out her phone and sent a group text to her sisters.

Maybe I don't understand men because I don't have any brothers.

The message went zipping through cyberspace, where it would land on her sister's phones. They'd send back condolences about Jeremy, who Eden had been very hopeful about. Then they'd throw in stories of their latest dating disasters, and Eden would offer to make dinner at her place that night.

She'd always felt a bit out of place among her sisters, but they were her best friends at the same time. She wasn't sure why her parents had gone for plant names for all of them, but she'd gotten Eden.

Orchid, Iris, Ivy—and Eden. It might have made sense if she was the baby of the family. Like the Garden of Eden. But nope. She was the second oldest, and the twins—Iris and Ivy—had just celebrated their thirtieth birthday.

The sky darkened, and Eden glanced up. Concern flowed through her, and she realized she'd been staring at her phone instead of paying attention to the weather. Things could shift suddenly out in the ocean, and she knew better than most. How many times had she said that to tourists coming through the office?

Thousands.

She hastily stood up and packed up her things, the first drops of rain already falling though the sun was still shining in parts of the sky. She'd climbed for a good hour before stopping, and it would be slick and hard to get down if the rain continued for very long.

Big, heavy drops kept pounding the ground around her, soaking her face and hair before she'd even shouldered her pack. What a perfect way to end this horrible week, and it felt like God and Mother Nature had combined forces against her.

She took a few steps to the corner and hesitated. Perhaps she should just stay here. One step into that wind, and she might blow away. Her calves burned from standing on the downward slope, but she couldn't see very far behind her to know if there was a cave or a small divot in the rocks where she could at least find some shelter from the storm.

Most storms like this raged for fifteen minutes or less, and if she could just wait it out, she'd have a much smoother hike back to her car.

Turning, she headed back the way she'd come, passing the flat spot where she'd eaten lunch. She kept one hand continually on the cliffs on her left, her situation growing more and more dire by the moment.

She finally stopped, unable to keep climbing due to the slope and the slippery mud the path had become. Feeling stupid—how lame would a headline look about one of Getaway Bay's top outdoor tour guides getting stuck in the wilderness?—she pulled out her phone and texted her sisters.

Stuck out a Bald Mountain Cliffs. If I don't call someone in an hour, send help.

Help? Orchid's text came right back, and Eden tried not to roll her eyes. Orchid never wore anything but heels, the thought of actually hiking a horrifying one.

Eden couldn't focus on the text string right now. She needed to get out of this rain. After zipping her phone back in her pants pocket, she turned back down the trail. Maybe she'd missed something, but it was pretty hard to tell.

In the end, she crouched down close to the face of the cliff and ducked her head as low as possible, covering it with her hands. The storm would just last a few more minutes. Microbursts. That's all Hawaii got, unless they'd already braced for a tropical storm or a hurricane. And there hadn't been anything on the weather report that morning.

She wasn't sure how long she crouched there, but it couldn't have been long—her knees didn't even hurt yet—before an awful, cracking, crashing, thundering sound filed the air. Filled her ears, her whole soul.

She gasped and lifted her head, trying to locate the source of the noise. But it echoed from everywhere, as if the sky itself had split open and the Earth would be ending in the next few seconds.

The warm rain pounded against her face, blinding her, and Eden ducked her head again, true fear flowing through her.

The ground beneath her began to shake, and she bolted to her feet.

"The mountain is coming down."

Sure enough, in that moment, Bald Mountain Cliffs started shedding off rocks like a snake does its skin. Eden had nowhere to go to escape—not this time.

She got swept away by the landslide as it rammed into her back, stealing her breath and shooting toward that corner she'd rounded. She knew the landslide wouldn't turn and follow the path, but go right off the side of the cliff.

And she was going with it.

She screamed as she fell, landing much sooner than she'd have thought. She rolled as more mud and rocks continued to rain down on her, pain flashing through her temples, her knees, her back, and her hands.

All at once, she found shelter from the rain and all the debris flowing over the path above. She drew in a shaky breath, the edges of her vision turning white.

"I'm going to pass out," she murmured, glad she'd texted her sisters.

"Hey," a man said, and Eden jerked toward the voice. Bad move. Her head swam, and she couldn't see very well at all.

She groaned and started to tip forward, the man catching her in his arms at the same time he said, "Eden?"

Eden looked up in the gorgeous, if not a little bloody, face of Holden Holstein. Ah, Holden. This was a nice dream. One where he held her in his arms, kissed her, shared his deepest sorrows with her.

"Are you with me?" he asked, and Eden's eyes snapped open again. "Don't pass out, Eden."

But she couldn't hold on. Of course Holden—the one and only man she'd ever loved—would have to be in this cave. Had to be a witness to her falling off a cliff and passing out.

"Holden," she murmured. She'd wanted to say so much to him before they'd broken up all those years ago. But she couldn't then, and her tongue was too thick and her brain too slow now.

So she settled into the warm darkness, the scent of Holden's skin and cologne lulling her right into unconsciousness, the way it had so often in the past.

———

Ooh, a landslide and an ex-boyfriend and MORE Getaway Bay Romance. Yay! **Read THE PERFECT STORM today!**

BOOKS IN THE GETAWAY BAY RESORT ROMANCE SERIES

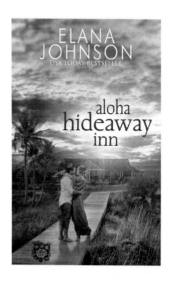

Aloha Hideaway Inn (Book 1): Can Stacey and the Aloha Hideaway Inn survive strange summer weather, the arrival of the new resort, *and* the start of a special relationship?

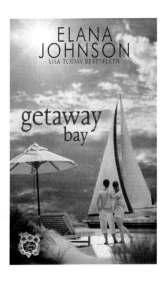

Getaway Bay (Book 2): Can Esther deal with dozens of business tasks, unhappy tourists, *and* the twists and turns in her new relationship?

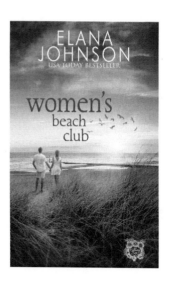

Women's Beach Club (Book 3):
With the help of her friends in the Beach Club, can Tawny solve the mystery, stay safe, and keep her man?

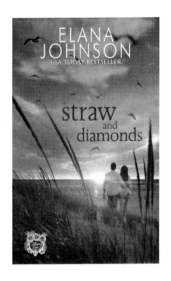

Straw and Diamonds (Book 4): Can Sasha maintain her sanity amidst their busy schedules, her issues with men like Jasper, and her desires to take her business to the next level?

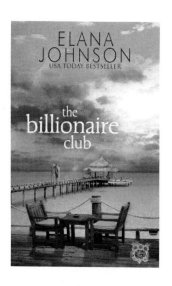

The Billionaire Club (Book 5): Can Lexie keep her business affairs in the shadows while she brings her relationship out of them? Or will she have to confess everything to her new friends...and Jason?

Sweet Breeze Resort (Book 6): Can Gina manage her business across the sea and finish the remodel at Sweet Breeze, all while developing a meaningful relationship with Owen and his sons?

Rainforest Retreat (Book 7): As their paths continue to cross and Lawrence and Maizee spend more and more time together, will he find in her a retreat from all the family pressure? Can Maizee manage her relationship with her boss, or will she once again put her heart—and her job—on the line?

Getaway Bay Singles (Book 8): Can Katie bring him into her life, her daughter's life, and manage her business while he manages the app? Or will everything fall apart for a second time?

Turn the page to view series starters from three of my other series!

BOOKS IN THE GETAWAY BAY ROMANCE SERIES

Escape to Getaway Bay and meet your new best friends as these women navigate their careers, their love lives, and their own dreams and desires. Each heartwarming love story shows the power of women in their own lives and the lives of their friends.

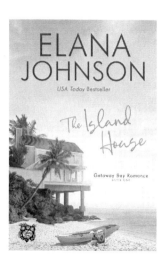

The Island House (Book 1): Charlotte Madsen's whole world came crashing down six months ago with the words, "I met someone else."

Can Charlotte navigate the healing process to find love again?

BOOKS IN THE STRANDED IN GETAWAY BAY ROMANCE SERIES

Meet the McLaughlin Sisters in Getaway Bay as they encounter disaster after disaster...including the men they get stranded with. From ex-boyfriends to cowboys to football stars, these sisters can bring any man to his knees when the cards are stacked against them.

The Perfect Storm (Book 1): A freak storm has her sliding down the mountain...right into the arms of her ex. As Eden and Holden spend time out in the wilds of Hawaii trying to survive, their old flame is rekindled. But with secrets and old feelings in the way, will Holden be able to take all the broken pieces of his life and put them back together in a way that makes sense? Or will he lose his heart and the reputation of his company because of a single landslide?

BOOKS IN THE HILTON HEAD ROMANCE SERIES

Visit the South Carolina Lowcountry and picturesque Hilton Head Island in this sweet women's fiction romance series by USA Today bestselling author, Elana Johnson.

The Love List (Hilton Head Romance, Book 1): Bea turns to her lists when things get confusing and her love list morphs once again... Can she add *fall in love at age 45* to the list and check it off?

ABOUT ELANA

Elana Johnson is the USA Today bestselling and Kindle All-Star author of dozens of clean and wholesome contemporary romance novels. She lives in Utah, where she mothers two fur babies, works with her husband full-time, and eats a lot of veggies while writing. Find her on her website at feelgoodfictionbooks.com

Made in United States
North Haven, CT
11 June 2023

37489594R00162